I0445787

What She Doesn't Know

by Lina Gardiner

Copyright © 2012 by Lina Gardiner

Lina Gardiner

On an Island
In an Ocean
Lies a Castle
Heart's Devotion

King and Queen
And Golden Princess
Behold their Realm
With Guarded Interest

Beyond the Sea
Beyond the Wall
A Name that Doesn't Suit
At all

The Key Becomes
For those who Seek
The Answer to its own
Mystique

CHAPTER ONE

RAVEN GALE made a huge mistake coming to this isolated island in the Bay of Fundy, on the East coast of Canada.

Whatever made her think she could track down the man who professed to be her dead husband?

Unfortunately, the thought of coming face-to-face with this imposter had been a lot less ominous in the daytime. But now, as the sun had set and the last rays of light disappeared below the thick canopy of trees, her misgivings were growing as fast as her insect bites.

And speaking of misgivings, she'd hired a guide to keep her safe, just in case. Captain Mike swore he knew the way to the house. But, they'd been wandering in the woods for hours and rather than listen to her he kept weaving his way through the forest in search of non-existent paths. They'd probably been going in circles.

"Where is the house, Mike?" she asked, fatigue weighing down on her. Neither of them had brought any water and she was parched. Her so-called guide probably had no idea how to even make his way back to his boat. She was about ready to mutiny.

"Hell if I know. I hate this damned island." He grumbled something nasty under his breath. It would give her great pleasure to fire him right now, but being lost in the woods on an island, miles off shore, didn't leave many options. Not to mention Mike's boat was the only way back to the bigger island of Grand Manan.

She'd almost given up hope when a gust of wind rustled some leaves in front of her and a pinpoint of light sparked through the foliage.

"I see a light," she shouted and stumbled forward through the brush in such a hurry that a spruce bow whipped across her cheek. It stung, but didn't slow her down until she broke through the tree line into an open hay field. She pressed her fingers against the welt and stopped to catch her breath.

Behind her, Mike yelled for her to wait. Like she'd listen to him now. He'd been so rude since they'd gotten lost, anyway.

At the sight of the old two-story unpainted farmhouse sitting on a cliff overlooking the ocean, she felt a dark, cold thing that resembled fear skitter in her belly, but it was too late for regrets.

"Where the hell did you go, Mrs. Gale?" Mike shouted while crashing through the woods on a dead run in her direction. He sounded like a wounded moose until he stopped beside her and started coughing. "Cursed island, if I never see this place again it'll be too soon."

She ignored his comments.

"You shouldn't have come here," Mike said unexpectedly jamming something hard into her ribs.

"Ouch! That hurt." When she saw the barrel of a gun, her legs turned to sponge. "What are you doing, Mike? I don't understand."

"Start walking. Now!" he said. "Can't see why you're complaining, I'm going to make sure you meet the man you came here to see."

The tone in his voice sent chills up her spine.

"Now move."

She stumbled over the scruffy lawn toward a weed covered gravel path leading up to a set of twisted front steps. Terror blocked her ability to think straight. She'd finally stepped outside her secure little world and look what happened.

"Open the damned door—move it."

Before she could get it fully open he shoved her inside. Bastard! She stumbled over the threshold and nearly fell.

It had seemed like such a good idea to hire a guide for

protection. How could she have known he worked for the imposter?

His meaty fingers dug into the soft flesh under her arm and he shoved her further into the foyer.

"What are you doing here, Mike?" An angry voice said from the other end of the hall. A man stood in the shadows, just far enough away that she couldn't see him clearly.

"Barry?" Mike said, "That you? Look who I found on Grand Manan. She even paid me to bring her to you." He pushed her forward. She stumbled again but somehow managed to stay upright.

"Barry?" she whispered. It couldn't be. She tried to breathe but her lungs wouldn't work right now. In the back of her mind an irrational fear that it might really be him, her supposed dead husband, fueled her expanding panic.

When the man stepped out of the shadows, his familiar dark hair, broad shoulders, and that face—she felt instantly numb, it was as if the floor suddenly had no substance under her feet. Maybe his build wasn't quite right, but it had been a year since she thought she'd buried him. Because her knees could no longer be trusted, she grabbed at a side table to keep herself upright. The table didn't help. For the first time in her life blackness engulfed her and she felt herself falling into a mindless oblivion.

* * * * *

Sloan barely caught her on time.

"What the hell is going on?" Sloan Brockway aka Barry Gale snarled at Mike. The idiot would have let Raven collapse onto the hardwood without lifting a finger. Damned thug.

Raven's limp form draped across Sloan's arm, her long

blonde hair, in direct contrast to her name, felt silky against his skin. Dressed in clam diggers and a T-shirt, he could see she'd lost weight in the last year. He gritted his teeth and glared at Mike. "How'd she get here?"

"I brought her," Mike sneered. "She was hell bent on finding you, Gale," he said sarcastically. "And, here's an interesting tidbit, the broad says she has business with you. Now, I'm wondering what kind of business this little lady would have? No one is supposed to know we're here." Mike ended his rant by poking Sloan in the chest.

"Back off, Mike." He'd only get one warning. Dumb-ass.

"Mister Brimm don't like double-crosses," Mike said, oblivious to the slight tick beginning over Sloan's left eye.

"What are you talking about? I've never seen this woman before. Take her back to Grand Manan before the others see her."

Mike snorted. "That why she fainted when she laid eyes on you, Barry? Never seen you before?"

Sloan knew why she'd fainted. From a distance he'd caught her off guard. He looked enough like her dead husband to be able to pull off this pretence, but he never expected her to show up here. She was supposed to be home in Chicago.

As far as he knew, she rarely moved outside of her safe zone. In fact, after Barry's funeral, Sloan had predicted she'd crawl further into her shell and not venture out again for a very long time. Unfortunately for her, she'd been way more resourceful than anyone expected.

"Help me get her into the den."

Mike didn't budge. He wasn't overly energetic at the best of times as far as Sloan could tell.

"I'm tired. I've been lost in those damned woods for hours. Why do you want help to get her into the den, anyway? Just leave her on the floor until she comes around?"

Sloan exhaled sharply. "Because, we need to get her out of the main hall. And we need to decide what to do with her. After all, you're the one who brought her here. Brimm is not going to be very happy with you."

The idiotic grin slipped off Mike's face. "What do you mean? I had to or she would have just got somebody else to take her."

"Think that's how Brimm'll see it? Maybe he'll say you shouldn't have told her we were here in the first place. You realize she'd have had no idea how to find this island unless you told her about it."

Suddenly Mike wouldn't make eye contact. His skin had turned a pasty gray hue. "I didn't tell her," he lied.

"Really? No one on Grand Manan Island knows me. She would have just asked around and then gone home empty handed — if you'd kept your trap shut, that is."

Mike swallowed hard, and his eyes widened. His pupils dilated. "Ah, hell."

"Got yourself in a load of trouble, buddy. And nobody can help you out of it. Especially not me." Sloan shook his head. Schmuck.

Even an idiot like Mike knew Brimm wasn't a man to mess with.

Mike stumbled to the desk and leaned against it, his chest heaving and his eyes moving back and forth while he tried to figure things out. Luckily he wasn't paying the slightest attention to Sloan as he lowered Raven onto the antique chaise. Nor did he see Sloan grab the brass lamp. He silently apologized then hit Mike across the back of the neck in just the right spot. The thug never knew what hit him.

Ten minutes later, Sloan slipped into the study and clicked the lock on the door as silently as possible. He pulled the desk drawer open, lifted out the false bottom and extracted an untraceable cell phone and dialed.

"Johnson, it's me."

"Sloan.   I'm sorry to report Mrs. Gale has disappeared."

"Yeah, well hold onto the reigns, because she didn't disappear—she's here." Sloan rubbed one hand over his eyes and leaned back in the solid wood executive chair. His glanced at the beautiful furniture in this abandoned room and wondered what it would be like to work in a great place like this—without thugs congregating down the hall, and without a woman tied up in the pantry. Things couldn't get much worse.

"You're lying," Johnson sputtered from his end of the line.

"Wish I was.   But, no, I'm honest-to-God serious. She's here."

"I can't believe she'd show up there on the island with you and Jason Brimm."

"You're telling me!   It's not something I'm happy about," Sloan said. He considered getting Johnson to let The Protectorate know about her being there but then hedged on that thought. The North American Protectorate had only let him back into the fold because they needed him. He'd keep this latest development to himself, and wouldn't report to them until he knew the whole story, and knew for sure he could trust them. After all, they'd thrown him out without a second thought a few years ago. His family might have respected this group their whole lives, but currently there were questionable people at the reigns.

Since Sloan hadn't been able to find the damned artifact everyone wanted, he desperately needed help right now. Maybe Raven Delacoeur/Gale would be his first break.

"I can't believe she's there," Johnson said again.

Sloan silently agreed. After Barry's attempt on her life a year ago, they'd kept Raven in their sights. And she'd never once gone outside her safe zone.

Sloan cleared his throat. "Question is how did she find me?"

"She hired a PI some time ago. I did a background check on him and by all accounts he wasn't exceptional."

Sloan cursed. "Guess he got lucky then."

"I don't know what to say about Ms. Gale, sir, she rarely leaves her apartment, except to go to work. I sure didn't expect her to bolt."

"She's not what I expected either and I'm not in the least amused by her sudden curiosity. Don't sweat it Johnson, there was no way you could've known she'd do something this out of character. Now that she's here though, I'll have to make her my priority. Which means, we'll have to push our main agenda to the back burner." Not something that pleased him, either.

"What's she looking for?" Johnson asked.

Sloan thought for a moment. "Barry tried to kill her. She probably wants to know why. Matter-of-fact, I'd like to know why, myself."

"True, but having her there is damned dangerous for both of you."

"All I can say is it was lucky she passed out when she saw me standing at the end of the hall. Wouldn't have been good if she'd called me an imposter." Sloan paced to the door and listened for sounds in the hallway before sitting behind the desk again.

"Do we continue our plan as discussed? Or, given the circumstances, do you need me to call The Protectorate to get you both off the island safely?"

"Not yet. If Barry gave these thugs information about the artifact he's definitely broken his family's sacred pact to The Protectorate. That has to be why Brimm and his men showed up here. I'm close to finding out what Barry told them. Listen, for now do not apprise The Protectorate of our situation. I'm not ready to fill them in yet. And while this is complicated enough without a babysitting job on the side, I can keep Mrs. Gale safe until I'm done." His gut clenched. He'd protect Raven with his life.

"Ten-four, Sloan. I'll be waiting for your directions."

Johnson didn't work for The Protectorate in the same way Sloan's family had. He was on Sloan's payroll and had been indoctrinated on Sloan's say-so. "You do that, kid. And listen— watch your back. I've learned that Brimm's got a few men working on finding Raven. All of a sudden they badly want her dead. Can't figure out why, but if you're asking too many questions they might get curious about you."

"That doesn't make sense," Johnson said, and by the tone of his voice Sloan knew he'd screwed his face up in his usual quizzical look. He was nearly thirty-five, but with his wire-rimmed glasses and his spiked haircut, he looked like he was still in his twenties.

"You're telling me. First Barry tried to kill her—why? And now this gangster wants her dead, too." He made a low whistling noise through his teeth when he was really worried, and he did it right now. "I can't figure it out. What possible reason would they have to kill her?"

"I guess that's the hundred million dollar question," Johnson said vaguely.

Sloan jerked forward in his seat and pressed the phone tighter to his ear. "By God, you're absolutely right, Johnson. It just might be the hundred million dollars, or whatever the artifacts are worth. That's why they want her dead. Find out who inherits if she dies, will you? And do it quick, we really need to know."

Sloan hung up and hid the phone again. He'd taken a chance making the call with the others so close. Who inherits upon Raven's death? Who got everything?

Opening the walnut door, he looked left and right before stepping into the hall.

A rumble of voices emanated from the living room.

He sauntered toward the room preparing himself internally. With shoulders straight and facial expression expertly set to tough, he entered the fray.

"Where have you been, Barry?" Jason Brimm gave him a suspicious once over the second he entered the room filled with thugs who looked like they belonged in a "B" movie.

"Do I have to report my whereabouts every minute?" Sloan asked, keeping his voice tough.

From his high-and-mighty position in the chair by the fire, Brimm tipped his head back and squinted at Sloan then angrily snapped his short fingers. Two goons pounced.

Sloan had no delusions. Neither of these men would give a second thought to killing him. In fact, they'd probably get a bonus for the job. Their dank, soulless eyes were proof of their ability to do the deed without losing any sleep.

Weakness wouldn't be tolerated by these low-life predators—Okay by Sloan, he had a difficult time playing his sniveling cousin, Barry. He'd spent his whole life proving he was tough and capable and nothing like his relatives on that side of the family.

"I went for a run," Sloan lied and snagged a bottle of beer from the table. In actuality he'd lugged Mike to an outbuilding where no one was likely to find him. And, since he didn't have time to wait until Raven came-to, or to convince her he wouldn't hurt her, he'd tied her up and left her in the pantry until he could get her to a safer location.

"I told you not to leave the damned house when you're working on my dime," Jason Brimm said.

A bead of sweat rolled down the side of Sloan's face. He'd had quite a workout getting Mike out of the way. The guy weighed a ton.

"Yeah, I know. But, we've been cooped up here for a week straight. A guy gets edgy on an isolated island."

Maybe Brimm would believe that kind of logic. Besides, how could Sloan find the hidden artifact holed up inside this musty old house?   It didn't make sense...Unless! Unless Barry told Brimm the artifact was inside. It was in the house, but where?

"Regardless, I expect people on my payroll to do what I tell them to." Brimm's hand went into his jacket pocket, indicating he had a weapon and was ready to use it. Sloan wasn't afraid since he knew it was an idle threat, because Brimm needed him. Nevertheless, he'd have to play his part well or Brimm and his thugs would get suspicious.

"Keep up your end of the bargain or you'll regret it. Don't forget most people don't like the way I exact payment if they fail to play by my rules," Brimm said. He pulled a cigar out of his breast pocket, bit off the end and spat it onto the amazing old hardwood floor.

Sloan gritted his teeth. "Understood."   He had to pretend to bow down to this jerk.

Brimm squinted at him, assessing him in a way that made Sloan edgy. Sloan would have to watch his attitude in future. Last thing he needed was to give himself away, especially with Raven here.

Brimm's beady eyes sparked with distrust. "Just don't get the idea that you can do this on your own. My partners sign in blood and you're in-to-me for twenty G's."

Of course he was, probably gambling debts. Sloan held back a sound of irritation that threatened to erupt. "I'll find the treasure. It just might take a little longer than you expect."

The way Brimm's jaw clenched and his eyes narrowed reminded Sloan of a predator about to attack. "Don't get any ideas about double-crossing me and keeping the treasure, Barry," he said.

"No reason to double-cross you," Sloan lied. "Besides, I want my piece of the pie."

Sloan must've said the right thing, because suddenly

Brimm's shoulders relaxed, he picked up a bottle of scotch and poured three fingers for himself. Bodyguard number two, Cyril, like a good lapdog, put ice in the glass and stepped away.

"Drink, Barry?"

"Already got a beer." Her held it up between two fingers and dangled it from side to side.

"That's soda pop. Real men drink Scotch."

Pressure on to conform as one of Brimm's subservients, Sloan set down his untouched beer bottle and poured himself a glass, about half as much as Brimm had. He took a drink of the vile liquid and grimaced. God, he hated Scotch, but Brimm was the boss, at least in his own mind. He'd brought two cases of fourteen-year-old stuff with him and he drank it like water.

"Drinks all around, boys," Brimm said. "We're alone on this island and since Barry here is on the brink of discovery, I'm giving you men a much needed break tonight."

Sloan gravitated to a chair in the corner and pretended to drink with them while he watched them getting more and more loaded.

He had to swallow some of the foul liquid, but he made sure he didn't drink enough to lose his edge. He'd wait for everyone to get drunk. Once they got wasted enough he'd have a chance to get Raven out of the pantry where he'd stashed her.

He thought he'd imagined every scenario on this assignment, had every eventuality planned, but he never once considered that Raven would come here, of all places. Since Barry's attempt on her life and his subsequent death, she'd locked herself up tight.

Hell. Sloan raked his fingers through his hair and imagined what it had taken for her to come here. But why, all of a sudden, did she need to find out what was going on?

Brimm crossed his arms over his expansive chest showing one meaty wrist covered with a thick gold bracelet. "You'd better be right about finding treasure, Gale. And you'd better not try to get away without giving me my share." His eyes were glassy and his voice slurred.

Geez, the guy was obsessive in his distrust. "I'll give you your cut. But we have to find the key to the artifacts first." That was the most honest thing Sloan had told Barry since he'd met him.

When The Protectorate had learned that Barry had conversed with Brimm over the phone before his death, they'd devised their plan to bring Sloan in as Barry. They kept the news of Barry's death out of the papers in the states, and since he'd died in Canada, nothing got back to Chicago. Even so, Sloan had been playing catch up ever since he stepped in. Bad enough he hated Barry Gale, but now he had to pretend to be him in the flesh.

Gritting his teeth, he thought about his not-so-dearly-departed cousin. They'd always been mistaken for each other, even in school. Since Barry was forever in trouble, even back then, being mistaken for him had gotten Sloan beaten up on more than a few occasions. That's when he'd learned to look after himself.

Barry had been in trouble his whole life, but being indebted to Jason Brimm had been his biggest mistake. These weren't the kind of people to borrow money from. And, now it was Sloan's job to figure out how much Barry had told them about the Protectorate and about the treasures they guarded. So far, Sloan had gleaned bits here and there, but not enough. He hadn't found any leads to where the artifacts might be. Not even a sniff. It might be a good thing Raven showed up when she did, she might be able to help him if he could convince her to trust him.

Meanwhile, Brimm's pea-shaped eyes narrowed and he leaned toward Sloan. "I'm not putting up with much more of your bullshit, Barry. I want what you promised me and you'd better make sure you find it by the first of next month or I'm going to turn you into an archaeological treasure, too." Laughter erupted amongst his thugs, feeding their boss's oversized ego.

"I'll find it," Sloan said between teeth locked together.

"You'd better or it'll kill you." Brimm curled back his ugly lips and drained his glass.

CHAPTER TWO

AN HOUR later, Sloan slipped into the pantry. He expected Raven to be afraid, but instead anger glittered back at him from those impressive eyes. Even tied up on the floor she hadn't lost her fight. Surprise—surprise.   Again he'd misjudged her.

He'd hated to tie her up and tape her mouth, but the last thing he needed was Raven Gale screwing up his job, or worse, getting herself killed on his watch. He crouched beside her and pressed one finger over his mouth to warn her to be silent.

"I don't know why you came here but you've inadvertently put us both in a very bad situation. Until I can get you away from here, you're going to have to cooperate with me. Do you understand?" He kept his voice soft, hoping she'd realize he wasn't the bad guy here.

She nodded, but she didn't mean it.   The minute he removed the tape she was going to scream her lungs out.

His chest tightened at the sight of those beautiful blue eyes that had entranced him from the first moment he'd ever seen her. It hurt a bit that she didn't recognize him.

"Here's the honest to God truth, Raven—if you make any noise, the others will know you're here and we'll both be in very deep trouble." He watched her expression closely to make sure she understood before he took the tape off her mouth. "Promise me, you won't shout."

She nodded vigorously.

Problem was, she had no reason to believe him, especially since he was the one who'd tied her up.

"Before I do this, I have to be sure. I understand that I

probably look like the bad guy given your current circumstances."

Those expressive blue eyes silently agreed with him.

His fingers grazed her hand near the tape and she jumped. "Here's my plan. There are six men across the hall. Four of them are hired guns. They've been given the night off and they don't get breaks often so they're making the most of it. They've been drinking for the past couple of hours. That'll give us a chance to get you out of here unseen. If I can get you upstairs, out of sight, you might be safe."

No denying the determination in her expression. And, she'd need determination to get through this mess, as long as she didn't alert Jason Brimm and his men.

Sudden shouting erupted across the hall. Sloan cringed at the sound of something breaking across the hall. The house was full of precious antiques and he'd hate to see anything destroyed, but the distraction created an opportune moment to make his point to Raven.

"It's me or them, Raven. Make up your mind right now." The shouting and cursing across the hall commenced again, only louder this time and ending in raucous laughter after it sounded like someone had fallen down.

He knew the second she chose him over the others. It showed in her expressive eyes. He carefully removed the tape and held a bottle of water to her lips. "Just sip it. Don't drink too fast."

She took a long drink before trying to speak. "Why are you doing this?"

"It's a long story, but until I get you off this island, the less you know, the better." And the sooner he got rid of her, the better.

* * * * *

Raven glared at him. Up close, he still looked a lot like Barry—maybe not exactly, but close enough. She'd definitely seen Barry in him for that split second before she'd passed out from dehydration and shock.

Now, he was watching at her as if he didn't know what to do with her.

She struggled against the duct tape that cut into her wrists. The strange part being she had it in her head that Barry might not be dead. She'd been in hospital after the accident and had missed the funeral. Upon learning the coffin had been closed, she'd grown even more suspicious. That's why she'd hired an investigator and when information turned up about this place, she had to come. She had to find out. For extra security she'd hired a guide but look how that had turned out.

At this point, she had to concede that Barry was dead since the man before her looked like Barry but wasn't him. But why would this look-alike pretend to be her dead husband?

"More water," she said, her breath raspy. She'd never been so thirsty.

He offered her the bottle again, holding it to her mouth and letting her drink as much as she needed.

When she tried to shift to a more comfortable position her legs felt like bands of rubber. Her own fault, she'd had no fluids all day. "Am I supposed to believe you're not one of them?"

Holding two fingers in front of her lips without actually touching them, he said, "I'm not going to hurt you. As for the rest of the men across the hall, I'll have to explain about them later. First, we've got to get you out of this room and in order to do that you need to cooperate. Promise me you'll do what I say."

"People know I'm here," she said.

"Do they?" He sounded skeptical. "For their sake, you'd better hope no one else comes here." He checked his watch then dropped his arm as if it were suddenly too heavy to hold up. "It's ten P.M., Raven; I know there's no boat coming for you. In fact, I had to take care of Captain Mike, myself. Where is his boat moored, by the way? It might be a problem if the others see it."

"You killed him?" Blood drained from her face and rushed to her toes.

"No, I didn't kill him. He's locked up where they won't find him for now only his surroundings aren't quite as comfortable as yours. Look, we have to get out of this pantry before someone stumbles in here. There's a back stairway to the bedrooms. Think you can make it?" He bent to remove the tape he'd used to bind her ankles.

She held out her arms for him to undo the tape on her wrists. Escape scenarios rushed through her mind. After her experience with Mike, it was highly probable the story was true about the men across the hall being dangerous.

"I'm sorry I had to do this to you," he said, removing the tape on her wrists.

She might have even tried to fight him off and run for the door if not for the increasing noise and shouting across the hall. She thought about the gun Captain Mike carried. Were they all like that?

"Let's get moving." Regardless of his size, he moved to the door with stealth.

She took the best option she had at the moment, and that was following him. If she saw any opportunity to escape, she'd make a break for it.

He inched the door open a crack, scoped as much of the hall as he could then motioned with two fingers for her to follow. It appeared he really wanted to get her away from the men in that room. But was it for her safety, or his own reasons? She shuddered.

They'd barely started down the hallway when a door flew open ahead of them. Her abductor grabbed her and pulled her into a shadowy alcove. She dared a glance at the heavy set, unkempt man, who staggered past. He was obviously very drunk. At the sight of the gun in a holster under his arm, prickles erupted across her flesh.

As if sensing her reaction, her abductor reached back and clutched her hand in his and whispered, "Shh."

Thankfully, the drunk returned to the room without realizing they were there. The instant the door shut again, her abductor released his hold on her hand.

"Okay, hurry before someone else decides to leave that room."

She'd found out one thing for sure. Mike wasn't the only man in this house with a gun and the story she'd just been told in the pantry now held an element of truth.

With this additional information, she weighed her options every step of the way up to the second floor. Obviously, her chance of finding an escape route just got a lot iffier.

She could scream. Fight. Run. But there was no doubt it would be foolish to alert the men downstairs to her presence. In fact, it might be the worst thing she ever did.

"Don't stop now," he said behind her. "Keep going."

At the end of the hall he dug a skeleton key out of his pocket and opened the door to a bedroom. She stepped inside reluctantly and saw one double bed, a dresser and very little else.

"It'll be okay." He clamped his hand on hers and pulled her further into the room. "Look, I've got to go back before they get curious and come looking for me."

"You're not going to lock me in here, are you?"

"You knew the risks when you came here, Raven. Now, I wonder if you're willing to do whatever it takes to stay in one piece?"

She shivered and he noticed—damn it.

"You should have dressed warmer," he said in an abrupt tone. "The weather here can be unpredictable."

As if she'd know that! She'd never been here before and certainly hadn't expected to stay.

His attitude ticked her off and even though she said, "I'm not cold." She crossed her arms over her chest and ran her hands up and down her bare arms to get rid of the chill bumps. "Besides, I don't intend to stay here as a captive in this bedroom, or on this island." She pushed her shoulders back to show more bravado than she felt.

What the hell had she been thinking coming here alone? She'd spent most of her life creating a risk-free environment for herself, and the one time she tries to use her backbone she ends up in the worst situation imaginable.

"Please just let me go," she managed to choke out.

An unreadable expression played across his features. Could've been regret. Could've been anger. She wasn't sure.

"All I can say is you're lucky I'm the one who found you and not Jason Brimm or his men downstairs."

So he kept telling her. Was she supposed to be grateful? He was locking her into a bedroom with no idea what he intended to do to her. She licked her dry lips and watched him back out of the room.

"Not one sound, Raven. Trust me and maybe I'll get you out of this in one piece."

Did he expect her to believe that? She frowned. "How do you know my name, anyway?" She certainly hadn't told him who she was. Had Captain Mike?

He paused, and for a minute looked like he was going to say something then changed his mind. "Later," he said and held up a hand to stop her from talking again. Don't let anyone know you're up here after I leave. "

"If you don't want me here, why don't you just let me go?" she said breathlessly. "I promise I'll leave right away."

"I'm afraid that's not possible now," he said, standing

in the hallway looking into the room—his shoulders rigid.

"At least tell me who you are?"

"Barry," he said through tight lips, eyes narrowing slightly as if to dare her to disagree.

"But, you and I know that's not true…"

His expression seared her. "Don't say those words aloud until I tell you it's safe to speak them. Do you hear me?"

She'd probably pushed her luck to its limit. Time to back down, just for now. "Yes… Barry."

Her sudden cooperation obviously surprised him, but he quickly regained his cool. "Smart girl. Now keep this door locked tight. If anyone tries to come in make sure you hide."

Panicking, she spotted a duffel bag in the corner. "Whose bedroom is this?"

"It's mine," he said in a tight voice.

Great, he was locking her up in his bedroom now. What would happen when he came back? She wiped her moist hands on her hips. She had to get out of here!

He started to close the door between them.

"Please don't lock me in here." The ancient skeleton key in his hand drew her gaze and a squirmy feeling assaulted her. Too bad she'd missed the class on lock-picking 101. Damn it.

"It's better that I have the key, for now," he said. 'It'll keep you safely inside and more importantly it'll keep the others out."

Holy hell, why did he have to keep scaring her? She was frightened enough. "Let me go, please." At this point she wasn't above begging.

"Don't try to escape. Even if you don't get caught, you have no idea what dangers lurk outside at night time." He clicked the door shut then turned the key in the lock from the other side.

She was locked in!

She slumped onto the floor at the end of the bed. Would anyone alert the authorities? She was on vacation from her job as a Librarian and she'd told everyone she was going away. Great. She wouldn't even be expected back for two weeks.

Glancing toward the single window in the room didn't help her sense of panic. The curtains were open a crack and she could see that thick fog had rolled-in since she'd been trapped inside this house. It wasn't cold in the bedroom, but a chill seeped into her bones nevertheless. Even if she could get out, she'd never be able to make her way back to the beach in this kind of weather. It had been difficult enough in daylight. Nor did she have any way to get back to the bigger island of Grand Manan, or the mainland.

She had very few options and given the fact that she was terrified of the ocean, she'd never make it back to shore on her own. She was in deep trouble.

The noises downstairs kept her nerves tightly strung. Every creak in the house made her think someone was coming.

It had to be well after midnight when she heard the key scraping in the lock. She dropped to the floor and slid quietly under the antique brass bed with her heart pounding double-time.

"It's only me," he said, locking the door behind him. "Come out from under there."

She slid back out and glared at him. His resemblance to Barry sent an icy cold barb through her heart every time she saw him.

The sight of the cold drink on the tray he carried made her mouth water. She was still dehydrated, no thanks to him. He could've at least left a bottle of water for her.

When he set the tray on the bed, she eyed the two thick brown-bread sandwiches and a tall glass of orange juice, hunger gnawed at her.

"Eat up. You must be hungry."

She glared at him and for the first time noticed he was soaking wet and shivering. In fact, water dripped from his sodden jeans and bare feet.

The boat! He'd been to Captain Mike's boat. He'd said he had to hide it, but why was he wet? Had he been swimming? An image surfaced from nowhere—black waves surging and ebbing, pulling bodies down into its depths.

"You're a little pale. You okay?" he asked.

"Oh, I'm just peachy," she said curtly. Her parents had drowned when she was a teenager and she'd been raised by a bachelor uncle who loved her but had no idea how to raise a young girl. She'd married a man who hated her and tried to kill her. And the piece de resistance, she was a hostage on a secluded island. What else could go wrong?

He squeezed some of the water out of his wet hair.

Panic burst through her veins in an adrenaline rush. She'd been trying to escape via the window but it had been sealed shut by layers of paint. With nothing more than a paperclip she'd found in her pocket, she'd failed to open the window on the second floor.

"You'd probably feel better if you ate something," he said.

"You might have drugged it."

One eyebrow rose and he took a drink from her glass then he picked up one of her sandwiches and pulled a corner off, popped it in his mouth, chewed it and swallowed. "Yum," he said with his mouth still full. "Not poisoned. Quite good, in fact."

She glared at him. "Hiding Mike's boat so no one can find me, is—is criminal! Where's my husband? And what's going on here?"

"Keep it down," he ground out. He pulled off one sopping sock and then the other. "Besides, you know your husband's dead.   I saw you at the graveside a couple of weeks after the funeral."

"You were watching me a year ago? You were at his graveside?"   It didn't make any sense.   "What possible reason could you have to impersonate my husband? Or to watch me?"

He sighed and rubbed his temples. "Look, it's late. I have to be up very early in the morning. Things are even more difficult with you here and I've got to get some sleep."

"I certainly don't think…" words clotted in her throat when he pulled off his T-shirt and unbuckled his belt.

Oblivious to her slacked jawed stare, he merely tossed the wet T-shirt into a plastic clothing basket in the corner then grabbed a towel from the dresser drawer and wiped his upper body down.

It'd been a while since she'd seen a man with his kind of proportions. Then again, maybe she'd never seen a man like him. Funny that she'd imagined he was Barry at first glance.   Their bodies were nothing alike now that she'd seen him without his clothes.

"Why are you taking your clothes off?" she demanded in a croaky voice, realizing how very much worse this whole thing could get, and soon.

"Isn't it obvious?" His lowered voice scraped over her raw nerves. "I'm getting undressed for bed."

"Wait! You can't!"

"Raven, you were married for God's sake, you're not going to see anything you haven't seen before."

Dread tightened her chest. Wanna' bet! Unlike Barry, this man's body was toned and tanned under his clothing. "It doesn't mean I want to see a stranger, like… like that," she stammered.

Disbelief dawned in his eyes. "You're not putting this on are you?" Jeans unzipped then removed and thrown on top of the shirt, he stood in front of her dressed in soggy Jockeys that left little to the imagination.

She steered her gaze away from him. "Just because I was married doesn't make me the kind of woman who'll jump into bed with the first man who drops his jeans, literally," she said, pulling her gaze from him to stare at the wet mound of clothes in the basket. "I don't know what you think you're going to do to me, but I'll tell you right now, I won't make it easy for you."

"Really?" The hint of amusement in his voice should have scared her; instead, it pissed her off.

Placing her feet strategically on the floor, she thought about the appropriate moves to stop an attack if she had to. If only she'd taken more than six Martial Arts classes.

He watched her stance change. "Before you pull a Jackie Chan on me, let's get one thing straight, I'm not interested in you. Got it? *NOT* interested." With that, he stripped off his underwear and pulled on dry ones.

Heat singed her face when he cast a wry smile her way. Why in the name of all that is holy had she been caught gaping at him while he changed?

He strode past her and turned down the bed covers. "Turn the light out before you get in, will you?"

"I'm *not* going to sleep with you in that bed. If you think I am, you're delusional."

He grunted, crawled into bed and settled comfortably into the pillow. "Where are you planning to sleep, then? Those men out there are killers, and rapists and God only knows what else. They'd love a naïve piece of flesh like you. If you want to be safe tonight, you'd better make up your mind to be quiet and let me sleep. If you don't, I can't be responsible for the repercussions."

Her mouth clamped shut. She thought about the men she'd heard downstairs. They had certainly sounded like the type of men she should avoid at all costs.

"You swear the juice wasn't drugged?"

"It's nothing but pure orange juice. Maybe I should have put something in it, though." He didn't bother to look at her, but could probably sense her horrified stare. "Relax, I'm kidding. It's only juice. Now, please finish eating and get into bed." He threw one arm across his eyes and exhaled.

She hunkered down on the floor at the end of the bed and hungrily ate one sandwich then wrapped the second one in a napkin for later, just in case she didn't get fed again.

He'd been quiet for a while so she jumped when he spoke. "Okay, Raven, you've caused me enough trouble by coming here, now get into bed and go to sleep or I'll pick you up and put you there, myself. And would you turn out the light if you're done eating?"

She got up and pushed the ancient, round electric light button and stood in the dark wondering what to do next.

"Who are you? What's going on here?" she asked. "How do I know you're not one of them?" Meaning the thugs downstairs.

She heard the rustle of linen when he lifted his head off the pillow. "Keep your voice down."

"Then tell me!"

"Believe me, I'm doing you a favor. If those men downstairs get their hands on you, the less you know about me, or anything related to this place, the better."

"If what you're saying is true, they'll kill you, too. So answer me! Why did Barry come here?"

He sighed. "How'd you find out about that?"

"Not that it's any of your business, I found a map to this island in one of his briefcases. After that, I hired a detective and he learned that Barry spent quite a bit of time here in the last year of his life."

"You're saying he left a paper trail? Sounds like something he'd do." Her abductor made a disgusted sound.

"Do you know, Barry?" She paused. "I mean—did you know Barry?"

"Yes. I had that unfortunate pleasure. But, I'll ask you again not to talk like that in this house. I'm Barry. Don't forget it." He sat up. "Look, Raven. I'm not going to hurt you. I'm trying to help you. Can you please, please just go to sleep? I can't tell you anything right now. For one thing I'm too damned tired, but the other thing is it's not safe to talk here. I promise I'll tell you more as soon as it's safe to do so."

"I'm just supposed to accept that?" she said, more to herself than to him.

"Last time Raven." He sounded calm, but serious. "You've come here and put yourself in this situation, now you'll have to play by my rules."

Inching toward the mattress, she didn't doubt that he'd carry out his threat to manually force her into the bed. He'd already trussed her up once.

After she slowly pulled down the covers, she wrapped herself completely in the blanket from the end of the bed before she got in.

"Good girl," he mumbled. "Now sleep. When you're with me you'll be safe."

Raven lay there in the dark, every instinct on alert. Awaiting the imminent attack.

It surprised her when he started to snore softly. He really had gone to sleep?

His breathing deepened. Hours passed. At least it felt like hours. She'd lain awake—on guard—listening for any sound, any movement. But nothing happened.

Not sure when her body decided to veto her mind on the issue of sleep, but finally she let go and dozed off. She'd nearly entered a dream state when his voice jerked her awake again. He was talking in his sleep. For the most part his mumbled words were completely unintelligible until she heard him say "They're dead. We've done our job, now we can go home."

Her eyes flashed open again and she bit back a scream.

CHAPTER THREE

THE NEXT morning Sloan rummaged through his knapsack, dug out a new toothbrush and left it on the side of the sink in the tiny bathroom built into what had probably been a closet at one time. He also left a note for her not to run the tap for very long in case someone heard it. Of course, he could've told her that in person but she was working so hard at pretending to be asleep, he left her alone.

First thing on his agenda was to grab her some food before anyone saw him. Hopefully, he'd made the right decision about keeping her here and not calling in The Protectorate.

Hell, he hated that she'd put herself in this position. If anything happened to her, it'd be more his fault by virtue of his genetics than anything else.

"Shit," he ground out between his teeth and jerked open the fridge door rattling the contents. Luckily, he noticed Brimm from the corner of his eye before he took anything out. Brimm had slipped silently around the corner and was leaning against the doorframe watching him. Sloan caked on his game face, but Brimm had already heard him cursing.

"Something wrong, Barry?" Brimm asked.

Crap. Brimm never got up this early and he'd probably mistaken the muffled curse for concern about not being able to find the artifacts. It was becoming increasingly irritating to have to continually convince a paranoid sociopath that he'd get his share of the prize.

"Nothing's wrong," Sloan said quickly shoving the three eggs he'd grabbed back into the egg crate.

"No? I think something is wrong. It's wrong that I have nothing to show for my time and money. As I said to you before, I expect results. I gave you a year to find the treasure without my interference, but now your time is nearly up." Brimm entered the kitchen and yanked out a glass from the cupboard. "I think we've established that I'm not a patient man. You told me if I backed you, you'd find the artifacts in a very short time, but so far—nothing. It's been too long."

"Yeah, but I'm close now, I'm sure of it." Sloan expected ranting after that comment but silence hung in the room with the weight of expectancy. Brimm went about getting some breakfast, and Sloan grabbed a muffin and ate it at the table. He'd have to get food for Raven later.

As tempting as it might be, it was too late to make a run for it, especially now that Raven had shown up. In fact, he wouldn't be working for The Protectorate right now if they weren't desperate. At least their desperation gave him a chance to dig deeper than they realized. It was the opportune time to find out what was going on.

In a way, he didn't blame them for the expulsion of the Brockway's. Barry's half-brother Victor had disappeared after he killed Raven's parents. The Protectorate figured Victor had drowned, too. His body had never been found. Then, Barry had the gall to find Raven and marry her to get at her family's portion of the protected treasure.

If Sloan hadn't been overseas fighting for his country at the time, he might've been able to stop their sham of a marriage. That alone stuck in his gullet. Worse, he looked enough like Barry to fool these thugs. He could see the pain in Raven's eyes every time she looked at him. He was nothing like her bastard of a dead husband, he would never be, but she didn't know that.

Then the stupid jerk had killed himself in the process of trying to kill Raven. At least he'd done one thing right.

Sloan shoved the last of his muffin into his mouth. It tasted like chalk. How could he ever tell Raven he was related to those men, but he wasn't like them?

* * * * *

Raven had pretended to be asleep when her abductor got out of bed and put on his clothes. After a couple of stolen glances at him, she shut her eyes and forced her breathing to sound normal. She heard the zipper on his jeans and when she heard the slip of fabric when he pulled on his T-shirt.

Her eyes squeezed even tighter shut.

He must've applied deodorant next because she heard the sound of a cover coming off and then the masculine odor of the stick. She doubted any of the thugs downstairs bothered with deodorant. Neither Mike nor the guy she'd seen in the hallway had been worried about cleanliness, so why was this guy different?

And why had he left her alone last night? Not that she was complaining. If he really wasn't one of the group of men downstairs, then who was he?

As soon as the door shut and she heard the skeleton key in the lock, she sat up and unwrapped her self-made security blanket.

She'd screwed up big-time. She had to get out of here, and it was about time she stopped cowering and started taking action.

First things first, she ate the second sandwich quickly then pulled back the drapes. Her spirits deflated when she saw the fog was just as thick as it had been the night before.

At least in the daylight she could see an old oak tree outside the window. An escape—a way down to the ground, but it wouldn't be easy. The tree wasn't as close as it needed to be.

On the upside, until her parents had drowned, she'd

been a tomboy. She might have changed after that, becoming more cautious and more afraid to try anything new but she'd have no trouble climbing down that tree—if she could jump the distance from the house. Big if.

With her face pressed against the glass to monitor how far it was to the ground, she said a quick prayer. What other choice did she have?

The window had still been stuck closed last night, but after digging at it with her paperclip for another half hour this morning, and with several aggressive shoves, she managed to push it open.

With a deep breath, she climbed up onto the sill and gauged the distance to the ground. From this vantage point, the tree looked even farther away. The reality of jumping faced her. Did she really have what it took to get herself out of danger? If she missed, what were her chances of survival?

She bit her lip.

There were two options, the men downstairs or the tree. The tree won.

Dragging in a long breath and ignoring the quiver in her chest, she hurled herself out the window and prayed she'd make it. She slammed into the tree—hard. Even though the air whooshed out of her lungs on impact, she grappled desperately and managed to gain purchase. She hung on while branches and leaves whipped past her at lightning speed while she careened downward. With a thump, and a moan she finally managed to snag a bigger branch. Once she was sure her arms hadn't been ripped out of their sockets, dazed and stinging from the scratches she'd gathered, she looped one leg over the branch and swung herself up, then worked her way carefully to the ground.

Dropping the last couple of feet, she brushed herself off and made for the forest. Limping, but feeling pumped over her death-defying feat, she hurried into the eerie, foggy woods. Could the dangers the imposter had warned her about be any worse than what she'd face in that house?

When she made it far enough into the forest to feel safe from anyone finding her, she sought the base of an old tree and curled up for a short rest. Cold fog, like a clammy hand, brushed the back of her neck. She shivered and wished she taken some of that man's clothing before she'd escaped. Why hadn't she thought of it? His duffel bag was back there in the bedroom.

The image of him sopping wet and stripping down in front of her, although distracting, reminded her that he'd hidden Mike's boat somewhere along the coastline. She had to find it.

Rather than go in circles this time, she'd travel in a straight line. One way or another, she'd find the coastline and Mike's boat. Since the imposter had moved it, she'd just follow the beach.

Teeth chattering, she stumbled through the forest until she heard the ocean and smelled the sea air. She managed to climb down to the beach over slippery rocks covered with seaweed without breaking her neck. Waves crashed onto the beach with fury while fog thickened the air with mists that swirled and muffled sound.

Where had her kidnapper put Mike's boat? And would she be able to see it in this fog?

"Lost, little lady?" An unfamiliar voice floated to her on the mist and she whirled around.

"Who's there?"

A stooped man in tattered clothes and a knit cap appeared out of the fog.

"Name's Davey. Who might you be?" When he got close enough that she could see clearly, she felt better. He didn't look like the same rough type she'd seen at the house. He had white, wispy hair and a scraggy beard. His matted, cable knit sweater had seen better days and his ragged brown pants were heavily frayed at the cuffs. He didn't look dangerous. If she'd seen him in the city, she'd think he was a street person. Maybe he was a hermit?

"My name is... not important," she said. No way would she give up her name if it were true that those people in the only house on this island wanted her dead.

His laughter sounded like a rusty door hinge with a wheeze at the end. "Come join me, I've got a little fire going inside. You're soaked to the skin, lass, you should have a jacket on."

"How'd you get a fire going in this? Everything's drenched." Her fingers could barely bend she was so cold. Waves crashed nearby and ended in a long, deep hiss as they caressed the shore.

"Found a little cave over this way. Some driftwood snagged inside and the stuff in the middle of the pile was bone dry."

If he belonged to the men at the house, wouldn't he be taking her back right now, not trying to get her warm? Plus, she was freezing.

Unless he had something under his sweater, he appeared to have no weapons. Not to mention he was ancient.

"In here," he said leading her through a slit in a rock face.

She had to duck in order to crawl inside. A few feet in she could stand. A fire blazed in the center of the dirt floor with the smoke escaping through a long thin opening in the top of the cave.

He smiled at her. In direct contrast to his rough, dirty exterior, his teeth were straight and white.

"Name's Davey O'Riley, miss." He dropped down onto the sand near the fire and patted the ground for her to join him.

"Do you live on this island?" she asked.

"No," he said. "Do you?"

Shivering to the point of barely being able to speak, she gritted out the word, "No."

She sidled up to the fire and held her hands out trying to staunch her uncontrolled shivering.

"Here, drink this," Davey said, handing her a mug of hot coffee from a nearby thermos. She didn't know where he'd made it and she didn't care, she took a gulp and enjoyed the warmth as it slid down her throat.

"You look familiar to me, lass," Davey said, taking a home rolled cigarette out of his pocket and lighting it with a thin twig he'd pulled from the edge of the fire.

"I'm not from around here, so that's not very likely," she said, downing the rest of the coffee. It was strong, exactly what she needed.

He eyed her up and down. "How'd you get so many scratches?"

She looked at herself. Stinging scratches zigzagged down both her arms. He probably thought she looked like she'd been rolling around in a briar patch. None of the scratches were deep, at least.

"Took a little tumble," she said, not bothering to tell him that tumble had been out of a window into an oak tree.

"Where'd you say you were from?"

She didn't, but since he wasn't going to let that question go, she answered. "Chicago."

"Ah, the windy city." He lit the cigarette with a twig, took two puffs then flicked it into the fire. "Never been to Chicago but I'd swear I've seen you before." He tapped his nicotine stained fingers against his chin. "You weren't here with a man several years ago? He had blond hair as I remember and a red beard that was hard to miss."

Raven's heart lurched. "That sounds like my father." She dropped onto the floor and dug her fingers into the hard packed sand of the cave floor. "The woman looked like me, you say?"

"Yes, but now that my addled old brain thinks about it, it couldn't have been you. You're too young. That beautiful young woman had your likeness though."

"Where exactly did you meet these people? On Grand Manan?"

"No, lass. Right here. Now that I think about it, it was a foggy day just like this when I met those two adventurers all those years ago. Least-wise, that's what they called themselves."

Raven sucked in a sharp breath. It couldn't be a coincidence that he'd met someone on this island who called themselves adventurers. Her parents had been here, but why?

And, if Davey had met her parents here years ago, then this might have been the ocean they drowned in. For some reason, her uncle would never tell her where it happened.

She didn't remember much from that time, either. In fact, she barely remembered going to live with Uncle Phil and most of the first year there had been a blur.

Even after she'd married Barry, Uncle Phil still wouldn't tell her where her parents had drowned. Raven hadn't pushed him because he'd lost his sister and he was grieving in his own way.

Now Uncle Phil was gone, too, and until this moment she thought she'd never find the place her parents had died.

Footsteps crunched outside the cave and someone shouted her name.

She jumped. Him! How had he tracked her here so fast?

"You'd best go, missy. Don't want no trouble. No one in that house knows I come here." The old man looked rattled and suddenly afraid. He jumped up and tugged at her shirt with one hand while his fingernails dug into her arm.

"Please let me stay," she said. "I'm afraid of the men at

that house."

Head shaking back and forth, he said, "You need to go! If they catch me, they'll make me leave."

"But they're dangerous," Raven said.

He nodded in agreement. "I've seen what they do to people." Haunted and maybe a little ashamed, he added, "I'm sorry but I can't help you, miss. If they find you here, we'll both be goners. Thing is, they won't stop looking until you're found. I can't take that chance."

"Don't worry. I'll go," she said. First-selfless-act. Crazy selfless act that would probably be the end of her, but at least she'd die knowing she protected the old guy. "Before I go, is there any way I can get off this island? Where is your boat?"

"Raven, where the hell are you?" The shouting was getting closer and more impatient.

Davey jumped nervously when he heard Raven's name being called again. "There's a boat arriving at six pm sharp tonight. They bring me supplies every couple of weeks. My friend will take you back to Grand Manan, but don't be late." He wagged a crooked finger at her. "And don't bring anyone else with you." He pushed her toward the mouth of the cave.

* * * * *

The image of Raven's broken body lying at the bottom of one of the many dangerous cliffs on the island spurred Sloan forward. If she'd been smart enough to leap out of the window and climb down that oak tree, surely she wouldn't wander off a cliff in the fog. But fog this thick could trick the mind, and she didn't know the island.

"Raven!" Cold, damp whorls of mist danced around him. Water droplets clung to his skin and made him shiver. Even wearing a sweatshirt over his T-shirt and jeans didn't help; he was still cold. With that flimsy outfit she had on she must be nearly hypothermic about now.

Worse, everything was slippery in this kind of weather. Beach stones in particular. She could easily fall and crack her head.

He remembered the first time he'd met her, he'd been asked to wait outside her house while his father had a meeting inside. Bored, Sloan had wandered around the corner and found Raven on a tire swing in the back yard. She had been barely sixteen and he was nineteen, but somehow before he left, they'd kissed.

Then his cousin Victor had gone off his rocker and killed her parents. After that incident happened, Raven had suffered traumatic amnesia. Her doctors had warned against pushing her to remember, so Phil made sure that didn't happen and none of his family was ever welcome to visit again. No wonder.

Besides, given his family connection to the worst disaster in her life, Sloan had no right to contact her. She'd forgotten him, anyway. But he never forgot her.

"Raven!" He shouted louder this time.

When she appeared out of the mist, her skin looked almost blue. She was soaking wet and Goosebumps were clearly visible on her arms and bare legs, even from where he stood.

He started to take off his sweatshirt.

"What are you doing?"

"You're freezing," he said.

She held up a hand. "I don't want your sweatshirt. I don't want anything from you, except a way home," she said and turned on her heel and started walking away.

"Hold up." He couldn't force her to take his sweatshirt, but he grabbed her arm without thinking. Her flesh felt like clay, and his first instinct was to wrap her into his arms to warm her.

Before he dared take that chance, she wrenched out of

his grasp and strode away from him. "Leave me alone."

He followed her. She'd injured her leg in the car accident when Barry had tried to kill her. She was limping again. It had been in the report that her ankle injury had been the most physically debilitating for her. The dampness probably made it worse.

"Come back here, Raven, you can't just wander around in the fog dressed like that, you'll freeze to death."

She slipped on a small stone and righted herself before he grabbed her elbow.

"Keep your hands off of me!"

He gritted his teeth. "I'm not the one you have to worry about."

"Said the spider to the fly," she grated, continuing toward a sand dune covered with scrubby grasses.

"If you're so intent on trying to make me believe I can trust you why don't you tell me what your name is? I can't go around thinking of you as what's-his-name, now can I?"

He couldn't keep her in the dark any longer, especially if he hoped to get her to help him. "You're right. You need to know what's going on. My name is Sloan Brockway but you'd better think of me as Barry for the time being."

"Not going to happen because I don't intend to be here once I find a way off this island."

"Even if you find a boat, how do you know you'd even head toward shore and not out to sea?"

That thought made her feel physically ill. Thank heavens he didn't know about her Plan B. She'd get off this island if she could make the six o'clock meeting with Davey and his friend. Forget trying to find out what was going on here. She just wanted to escape.

"Believe it or not, right now you're safer here with me than you would be at home in Chicago."

She whipped around and she narrowed her eyes on him. "First you knew my name, now you know where I live. Who are you, and why are you pretending to be

Barry?"

"It's a long story. One, we can't get into right now. Especially out here in the open. Suffice it to say, I'm on your side."

"Oh, okay, since you put it that way, I'll just trust every word you tell me from now on." She plunked down onto the sand regardless of how wet she got, and pressed her face into her knees.

Crossing his legs at the ankles, he dropped to the ground beside her. "Mrs. Gale, I wonder if you knew your husband as well as you thought you did?"

She sighed and looked away, her mouth a grim line. "Yeah, well, after he tried to kill me, I realized I didn't know him very well at all."

"Did you know he was a treasure hunter?"

Silence hung between them. She heard the words and rejected them almost instantly. "That's just a ridiculous statement, did you think that up all by yourself?"

He rested his forehead on his fingertips and stared at the sand underneath his sneakers. "To be honest, I didn't think Barry was capable of keeping his mouth shut long enough to hide the truth from you," Sloan said.

She thought about the possibilities of Sloan's statement being true. "I don't believe you. My uncle's house is full of old junk, some of it probably has value to a collector. After the first time Barry and I visited Uncle Phil together, Barry never went back. If he was a treasure hunter, don't you think he would've wanted to poke around?"

"Maybe your Uncle told him not to come back," Sloan said.

"Why would he do that?" And, why did she get the impression this guy knew Phil's name before she ever mentioned it?

* * * * *

Sloan bit off a curse. He'd better watch what he was saying. Raven had no idea that her uncle and her parents had been members of The Protectorate. Even though they'd spent their whole lives protecting ancient treasures, one very important treasure had been lost to The Protectorate when her parents had died.

"Just shows how much of a loser Barry was. He should've spent every spare minute with you." Sloan said.

Her cheekbones reddened with anger despite the cold. "And, how long did you know Barry?"

"Long enough to know what a son-of-a-bitch he really was," Sloan said.

"On that score we'll have to agree. He wasn't a prized human being." Raven wrapped her arms around herself and pressed her toes into the soggy sand.

"No, he wasn't. No one expected him to hurt you though?"

Her gaze locked on him and he couldn't look away.

"You say that like I've been the subject of conversation? Who would care about my relationship with Barry, other than my uncle, my last living relative? He's gone and I'm alone, now."

He nodded.

She composed her next question with more care. "So, you're telling me it really was Barry who died that night in the car accident?"

"That's the second time you've said that. What makes you think he isn't dead?" Sloan asked, running a hand through his wet hair.

Like she'd share her suspicions with him. He already knew way too much about her.

One thing about him surprised her, though, he didn't complain about sitting beside her on the wet sand. Barry would have had a fit by now. "Even if I believe what you just said, if he was a treasure hunter, why would he work as a travelling salesman?"

"It gave him cover. And a reason to be gone whenever he needed to be."

Since she'd married Barry she'd been his victim. He'd completely fooled her right up until the moment he'd tried to wrap her side of the car around a telephone pole to get rid of her. That was the hardest part to understand and probably the reason she couldn't let it go. She needed to know the truth.

"Please don't answer this question if you don't want to, but why did you marry him?"

Her laughter sounded cynical even to her. She narrowed her eyes on Sloan. "I made a mistake from day one and knew it. I was going to have our marriage annulled when Uncle Phil fell off his roof and died. After that, I was so distraught and alone I let Barry convince me that I needed him because there was no one else I could turn to. It was a stupid reason, but I really would have been alone without him." While she listened to the waves crashing on the shoreline, she'd just spilled her guts to a stranger and somehow it felt good to be rid of it.

Sloan cupped his fist over his mouth then said, "Raven. You're not alone. Don't you know that?"

She frowned at him. "Of course I am. I have been for a year."

He looked like he wanted to say something else, but clamped his lips together and stared off into the fog.

"Wait a minute. If you're pretending to be my husband that means you're hunting for the same treasure, doesn't it? How far would you go to get it?"

"I'm very determined to do my job and do it well. Finding archaeological relics is more than a job for me. For the most part I donate my findings to museums and universities." He pushed at the sand with his sneaker. "In my other life I'm a university professor."

University Professor? Somehow she believed that. No doubt his classes were heavily populated with females. She'd certainly never seen a University Professor who looked anything like Sloan Brockway.

"I'm assuming the proceeds of this particular venture won't be shared with museums and universities?" she said.

"No. This time I've got to work within very strict parameters."

"Is that how crooks say it these days? Very strict parameters?"

He mumbled something unintelligible, probably because he couldn't deny he was a crook. She jumped up and brushed wet sand off herself and started walking along the beach. "You know, you could've told me almost anything about Barry and I might have believed it, but treasure hunter?" She shook her head. "Not likely."

"Wait, where do you think you're going?" he asked.

"I'm searching for Captain Mike's boat."

"You'll never find it," he said. "I've hidden it."

She looked over her shoulder at him. "But, since I know you've hidden it, I'll be able to find it. This island is only so big, if I go all around the outside, I'll eventually come across it."

"Think you're smart, don't you?" Even though his words held a hint of sarcasm, he had a grin on his face.

"Not smart enough to stay away from this place, evidently. And, not smart enough to figure out what you're up to."

"You won't find the boat either, I'd wager. Fair warning, your method won't work."

The nerve! "I believe I might have mentioned this to you before," she said, smiling back at him. "I don't trust you! Therefore, I don't believe you."

He let out an exasperated sound and raised his arms in the air. "I give up. Go ahead. Try and find the boat, just make sure no one else sees you." He pulled his sweatshirt off and tossed it to her, then turned and headed back toward the house. He stopped just before the mists completely enveloped him. "Please don't fall off a cliff and kill yourself while you're searching."

"I'll do my best," she said, willing him to leave quickly so she could put on his sweatshirt. As she watched him fade into the fog, she yanked it over her head and snuggled into the interior while it still held his body warmth.

Was he really so sure she wouldn't find the boat, or was this a trick to psych her out? If it was merely a trick, he'd failed. She'd walk the perimeter of the island and she'd find that boat.

A few feet further down the beach Davey appeared on the dune. "He's right, miss. You won't find the boat. It's in a very secret spot. No one can find it, unless they know where to look."

"Do you know where to look, Davey?" She waited for him to come closer, noting that he appeared more nervous than the last time they'd met.

"If I wanted to, maybe. But I don't want to."

"Not even to help rescue me from these people?"

Davey assessed her, then closed his eyes and began mumbling something rhythmic under his breath. She couldn't make it out. "What are you saying, Davey?"

"You can trust him, you know—that man who just left. He's not like the rest. He will help you."

"Do you know him?"

"He doesn't know I'm here. You must promise never to tell him, or anyone."

Again Davey looked agitated, and she wasn't sure the upset was good for his health. He wasn't a young man, and probably not mentally-stable either. "How do you know he won't hurt me, Davey, if you don't know him?"

"I've seen him. He's good. He's not like the others."

"Where have you seen him? At the boat?" She thought she was being slick and could weasel the information out of him, but Davey simply frowned at her and pressed his lips tightly together.

"Okay, I'm sorry. I believe you. Now if you'll excuse me, I'm going to find that boat."

A branch snapped and Davey's jumped. "Wasting your time... "

She heard his voice floating on the mist and he was gone. Disappeared—just the way he had appeared.

He really must enjoy that fog trick, she thought to herself.

CHAPTER FOUR

SLOAN WANTED to follow her, damn it, but he couldn't. He had to show for breakfast or the thugs would get suspicious. And the minute he stepped back into the house he felt a weird vibe inside. Breakfast was in full swing, and thug number one, Paul, appeared to be cooking everything in the fridge, bacon, eggs, sausage, steak, there'd be no fresh food left tomorrow. Hopefully the dopes realized there were no grocery stores if they ate everything.

Six men sat around the large dining room table mounded with food.

"Pull up a seat, Barry. Have some breakfast," Brimm said. His plate was piled high with scrambled eggs, bacon, sausage, hash browns and steak. Ketchup flowed freely onto their food.

"Are we celebrating?" Sloan asked.

Brimm ignored his question. "Been outside again, Barry?"

"Just went for some fresh air."

Shoving in a mouthful of extra thick Canadian bacon, he said, "I'm wondering why you continue to disregard my orders? I asked you to stay in the house and do the job I told you to do. The boy's n' me are leaving today, so you'd better get serious and find the stuff."

"Staying in the house won't...." Sloan stopped himself before he made a big mistake. His heart started beating faster... Brimm had just told Sloan the artifacts were supposed to be in the house. Barry must have told him that, but he couldn't have found anything before he'd accidentally killed himself.

Brimm's head shot up when Sloan's sentence cut off.

His eyes narrowed. "You gettin' closer to finding it? You better not be trying to rip me off, punk."

If only Brimm would say exactly what he thought. Jerk!

Now that he knew Barry had narrowed his search to the house before he had died, Sloan was anxious to do a thorough search.

"I'm feeling positive about making some headway in the next few days," Sloan said, and this time he really meant it. He'd find the key to the artifacts now that he had an idea where to look. "I'm surprised you're leaving, though."

Brimm grunted. "Got another fish to fry in Chicago. I have more business ventures on the go than this one."

He was obviously seething under the surface. Someone was in deep trouble when Brimm got back.

"I'm leaving Preston here with you, so don't think you're going to get lonely."

Shit! Had he really imagined Brimm would just leave him alone to find the key, or the treasure? Not likely.

Brimm shared a knowing look with one of his thugs, a look that turned Sloan's blood cold. "At any rate, we're heading back to Chicago today. We've got other business to attend to," Brimm said.

The sense that things were off-kilter continued to build in Sloan's head, like a headache that wouldn't quit. The goal now would be to keep his wits about him and continue to play it cool to figure out the king pin's angle.

Grabbing some breakfast before it disappeared, Sloan sat at the crowded dining room table and listened to the men talk. One thing that worried him a great deal was the fact that Preston wasn't in the room. Where the hell was he?

When Sloan thought he couldn't sit here another second, Brimm lit a cigar and filled the dining room with smoke. "Gale, you help my men load the yacht. I'm sure

you won't mind since you like being outdoors so much."
He didn't wait for a response before he sauntered off.

   If Sloan hadn't been ordered to help the men move
their gear onto the yacht, he'd be out there trying to find
Raven at this very minute. He didn't like the thought that
Preston was on the loose on the island somewhere. What if
he'd already had found her—or for that matter, Captain
Mike. Was Preston looking for her? Did they know she
was here? Damn it!

   The sooner Brimm and his men were gone, the sooner
he could get Raven to a safer place and find out where the
hell Preston had gone.

* * * * *

   As predicted, the boat was nowhere on the coastline.
But, that didn't make sense. It had taken most of the day
but she'd walked the perimeter of the whole island, she
couldn't have missed it, especially since the fog had faded
away.

   The last thing she should feel right now was relief at
not finding the boat, but she *was* relieved, in a way. The
thought of actually having to take a vessel out onto the
water all by herself had her in knots. Besides, now that she
knew someone was coming here to deliver food to Davey,
she had an honest-to-goodness escape route. Her stomach
grumbled, and she wondered if she could find enough wild
berries and crustaceans on the beach to stay alive if she
missed the boat.

   Raven smiled widely when she spotted a yacht
anchored offshore. If her estimation was correct, the yacht
had anchored near the house. For a brief moment, she
thought this might be her way off the island, that the
occupants might be tourists stopping to look around, or
seeking shelter from the fog that banked just offshore. But,

from her sheltered spot on the cliff overlooking the ocean, it soon became evident it was the bad men carrying equipment down a winding path to the beach. They were loading their gear on board. Even from here she saw the guns on their belts. They didn't even try to hide them. She shivered.

A quick glance told her the tide had turned and fog was sliding back in again. Did it ever go away? It inched toward the island with insidious silence.

She whipped her wrist up to look at her watch. She'd been walking for hours and had nearly missed the time for Davy's friend to arrive on the other side of the island. If she wanted to make her boat ride out of here, she'd better hurry and get back to the isolated beach near Davey's cave.

By the time she made the rendezvous point, the fog had fully returned and its cold, dampness seeped into her bones. She rubbed the Goosebumps on her arms and was thankful for the hood on Sloan's sweatshirt. She managed to find the cave, but then panicked when it was empty. Where had Davey gone?

She tore outside and thought about calling for him but decided against it. She had no idea who might hear her.

No longer able to see more than a foot in front of her, splashing sounds echoed in the mists ahead. It was the sound of someone wading through the water. She tucked damp tendrils of hair behind her ears and sprinted forward. The outline of a rowboat came into view and two men stood beside it, one of them a familiar little man. Davey had four bags of groceries in his hands.

Relief almost made her limbs weak.

His eyes squinted when he saw her. "There you are. You nearly missed your ride. Burton was early today."

The rough looking sailor named Burton, reminded her a little too much of Captain Mike. "Do you mind taking me to Grand Manan with you?" she asked, yanking her wallet out of her pocket. "I'll be happy to pay you."

"I don't need your money," he said.

She hesitated and looked at Davey, not sure if she should say anything else.

"Cripes, Cap, the woman didn't suggest you *needed* her money. She merely offered you compensation for taking her back to the island."

Burton's chest deflated just a little and he looked embarrassed. "Sorry, lady. Didn't mean to be rude."

"Please, don't worry about it," she said. Not sure if that meant she should offer again. At least the next time she offered it would be on Grand Manan Island.

Someone cleared his throat behind her and she jerked around in panic. No!

"Just where do you think you're going?"

She'd recognize that voice anywhere. Barry's doppelganger was close enough behind her that she was fairly certain he could reach out and touch her. She resented the fact that he'd used Davey's trick and suddenly popped out of the fog.

Before she turned and glared at him for his cheap parlor trick, she noted the fearful look on Burton's face. Next she scanned for Davey. He was gone. For an old guy, he was quick.

Raven put her hands on her hips and stared her abductor down. "I'm leaving here, and you're not going to stop me."

"But that's where you're wrong, my dear, Raven. I am definitely going to stop you."

She resisted the urge to slap him. How dare he smile at her in that irritating way! How dare he tell her he was going to keep her prisoner when she had a viable escape route. He'd never get away with it. People knew she was here now.

He simply crossed his arms over his chest and planted his feet firmly on the sand. One look in the sailor's direction and a slight narrowing of his eyes caused a streak of curses to fly out of Burton's mouth. It seemed that the turtleneck sweater he'd changed into since she'd seen him last showed off his physique nicely, a little too nicely for Burton. He was backing away as fast as he could.

"Don't you dare leave without me," she shouted, suddenly desperate.

Burton, meanwhile, looked terrified. His head moved back and forth, then he turned and ran for the rowboat, practically propelling himself into it. He cursed to himself while he yanked the anchor up and began rowing.

In desperation, Raven ran to the waters' edge to beg him to come back, but Sloan grabbed her around the waist and lifted her off the ground.

"Put me down you jerk! Put me down!"

"Be quiet. You're going to ruin everything," he said in a low growl.

A quick glance toward Burton and her heart sank. He'd already disappeared behind the veil of fog. His oars splashing urgently as he hurried his escape. Coward!

The next time she saw Davey, she'd have something to say to him, too, for taking off and leaving her alone.

"Put me down." She sagged in his grasp.

The minute he let go, she turned on him. "How dare you keep me prisoner here, and from now on keep your damned paws off me."

His eyebrows shifted higher.

"Why don't you just let me go?" she shouted at him. So ticked at losing her escape route, she followed him along the path toward the house. "Tell me what's going on here."

His shoulders were taut and his steps forceful. "I wish I could. Believe me, I'm not in the least impressed to have you here. Might be a good thing for you though, because those thugs who left a while ago want you dead."

She stopped in her tracks. Even though she believed

the others were capable of murder, why would they have anything against her? "Me specifically? You're making that up to scare me."

He stopped, his expression serious. "Raven, who is the beneficiary of your estate?"

She cast a wary look at him. Was this a trick question before he killed her? "That's why you're so interested in me, to kill me to get my estate? Well, I'm afraid you're out of luck if that's what you think. There is no beneficiary, because he's dead. I named Barry as my beneficiary, at his prodding, I might add. But he's gone and Uncle Phil is gone. There's no one else."

"I don't want you dead." He huffed out a breath and looked heavenward as if she were trying his patience. "I'm the one trying to keep you alive, damn it."

She made a face of disbelief. "So you keep saying."

"Okay, look, Brimm is gone but he left one of his thugs behind. You're still not safe here and I still have to hide you."

"Know what, Barry…?" She drew Barry's name out and made it sound like an insult. "You keep telling me those other men want me dead, but not one of them has done anything to prove that to me."

"What about Mike?"

"Yeah, what about Mike?" she asked suspiciously. "Sure, he held a gun to my side, but after I passed out, I only have your word that he's in on this grand plan to get rid of me. If so, why didn't he just shoot me in the field out there? And now he's conveniently disappeared or should I say he's been hidden by you."

"I'll take you to him. Prove it to you," he said.

"Good idea. Lead on."

"Don't forget," he said as they made their way down the forested path. "Brimm left one of his men behind to make sure I find the artifacts. If he sees you, I don't know what he'll do."

She sighed. "So, I should stick close to you because I'm still in danger from yet another bad guy?"

"You have an irritating way of making me look like a liar," he said. "Just follow me, Mike will tell you the truth."

They were near the edge of the forest where the path opened into the hayfield. Sloan stopped in front of her just as she stepped over a tree root. About to ask him why he'd stopped, she spotted the thin man with a weasel's mustache, dead ahead and with a gun pointing at them.

Sloan slanted a look at her. It should have been a look of *I told you so*, but it was a look of concern. He put his hands up but his attention remained on her.

"Well this is a freaking surprise, now, ain't it? Brimm had no idea you were smart enough to bring her here. Kept her hidden the whole time, did you?" the man said.

"Look, Preston. This isn't who you think it is. It's my friend, Mary…. Mary Grant."

Preston laughed. "You're kiddin' me right? Do you think Brimm leaves idiots behind to make sure people are doing what they're supposed to? I know this is your wife." Preston spread his legs and took a dangerous stance. One hand steadied his other wrist, and he aimed the gun straight at her head. "I thought you were more than happy to be rid of your ball and chain? So why are you hiding her?" He snickered. "Been lying to Brimm about your feelings for her, have you?"

Raven managed to drag her eyes off the massive gun long enough to see Sloan's expression turn to ice. He looked like he wanted to murder somebody, but it wasn't her.

It seemed suddenly apparent, if she wanted to live, she needed to distract the guy with the gun and hope she didn't get herself shot in the process—but how?

"You don't have to do this," Sloan said and Preston's

attention shifted back to him.

"I'm sorry? What the hell's going on, Gale? Do you want her whacked or not?"

"Not!"

"That's too bad isn't it?"

"Wait, she can help me find the treasure. She knows where it is."

"You told Brimm she didn't have a clue. That, she had amnesia because of the accident." He scowled at her. "You saying she can suddenly remember?"

With the forest only two steps away, she could make the brush while his attention was on Sloan, she might get away. What other choice did she have?

"Preston! Think about this, if you cause Brimm to lose out on the treasure, he's going to be pissed." Sloan's voice resonated with authority and Raven realized he was distracting him long enough for her to run.

She did just that.

Panic spurring her forward, she tore headlong through the scratching, clawing thickets until a bullet whizzed past her head and slammed into a tree trunk to her left, she tripped and dropped to her hands and knees. Almost instantly another bullet hit the leaf litter nearby. Reacting quicker than she thought possible, she rolled to the right, got up on her hands and knees and dove head first over a large fallen tree, where she pressed against the dead trunk, breathing heavily.

Another shot sounded in the opening and echoed off the trees surrounding her. Next came the sound of the two men scuffling. There was a thud, and then a crack and all was silent. Her heart was beating so hard it vibrated her ribcage.

Who won the fight? Had it been Sloan, or the other man, Preston?

No way she'd go out there to find out, because she

wasn't going to move a muscle until she knew for sure.

"Raven? You okay?"

She listened to the voice. It sounded kind of like Sloan, but she wasn't sure. She hunkered down even deeper into the dirt.

"Raven, it's okay. Preston isn't going to shoot you. I need help to tie him up, though." There was a pause. "Shit, Raven, tell me that you're okay in there!"

That was Sloan. Definitely.

She pushed off the ground and peeked over the log.

From here she couldn't see the open field through the brush, so she crept as silently as possible toward the position where she'd heard his voice.

When she got close enough to see, Preston lay pinned on the ground with Sloan holding the man's arms behind his back. Preston struggled, but no way could he break the grasp Sloan had on him.

She moved out into the open and said, "What can I do?" She glanced around and saw the gun glinting in the grass a few feet away.

"I need to tie him up. Then I'll put him in the same outbuilding as Captain Mike."

At first glance she noticed that Sloan's left eyebrow had a cut over it, and his hair was messed. He was breathing heavily.

"I have to tie him up. Pull off his shoes and socks will you?"

"What? Why?"

"I'll use his shoe laces to tie his hands, and if he's in his bare feet it won't be as easy to get away if he makes a run for it," he said, tipping his head in the direction of the gun. "Grab the gun over there but be careful because the safety isn't on. Don't shoot one of us."

She felt a cold tingle of icy shards work their way up her spine at the thought of holding a loaded weapon and pointing it at a person. She yanked off Preston's shoes and socks, being careful not to get kicked. At this point, he didn't struggle much, mostly because Sloan shoved his knee into the small of the guy's back and applied pressure if he tried to move. She handed the shoelaces over and tossed the socks away before making her way toward the gun.

Cold, heavy plastic and steel made the gun feel heavier than it looked. She pointed the weapon at the ground and carried it to Sloan. The quicker she got rid of it the better.

Sloan took the gun from her and jumped to his feet with the gun pointed at Preston. Next, he yanked this man, who would have killed her, to his feet. Preston looked a little worse for wear than Sloan, he had one eye nearly swollen shut, and his lip was bleeding. It appeared they both got a few good cracks in before Sloan got the upper hand.

"You won't get away with this," he said.

Sloan shoved him and pointed the gun at him. "I'd better, or you're going to be very dead."

Preston turned pale. "Which way do you want me to go?"

Sloan pointed to an old stone building in the corner of the field, a storage-shed of some sort.

They got to the outbuilding and Sloan handed the gun to her again. "Keep this aimed at him while I tie him up."

"What if I shoot him by mistake? I've never held a gun before. I'm nervous."

Preston's eyes widened and he looked like he might upchuck.

Sloan caught the note in her voice and knew she was only half-joking. He winked at her. "Try not to kill him if you do shoot him. An arm or a leg would be better."

"Gottcha."

Preston hopped into the building quickly and Sloan shackled his ankle on the opposite wall from Mike.

"Let me the hell out of here," Mike yelled at them. "You're gonna' be so dead when Brimm finds out about this."

"You shouldn't complain, Mike, you've got water, and I bring you food once a day. What more can a criminal ask for?"

Mike cursed a blue streak and looked at Preston. "How the hell did you get caught? I thought you were Brimm's top man?"

Sloan took the gun from Raven again and he grabbed her hand. She didn't realize how icy cold her fingers were until his warm hand wrapped around them. They stepped outside and he shut the door on the men.

"Let's get back to the house," he said.

Raven instantly scanned their surroundings. Not that she could see far in the fog. "Why? How many of them are still here?"

"I think he's the only one. I saw the rest of the them get on the boat." He shrugged. "That's not to say they couldn't have dropped someone off on the shore around the corner, but I doubt they did."

"What's the hurry to get back to the house then?"

He eyed her up and down, his expression deadly serious. "You're turning blue for one thing. You're limping, and I've finally learned the artifacts, or the key or whatever the hell these thugs are looking for is in the house."

"Really?" Raven's heart skipped a beat. Was it excitement burbling inside her? It couldn't be. Surely someone who protected herself against such things, couldn't be enjoying any of this?

"I have one more question," she said looking back at the stone building.

"Yes?"

"Why would a storage building connected to an old house on an isolated island be equipped with leg shackles?"

He grinned. "The Bay of Fundy has all kinds of history, pirates, rum runners, who knows why the place needed shackles?"

She'd accept that for now. Obviously he didn't want to discuss why those shackles looked much less rusted than they should.

CHAPTER FIVE

ONCE THEY entered the house, Raven followed Sloan into the living room. He'd protected her out there. He'd jumped between her and the man wielding the gun. Not the actions of a mercenary who only wanted treasure, surely.

"Why do they want me dead?" she asked.

"I honestly don't know. It doesn't make any sense to me."

"Preston was going to shoot me. It just doesn't make sense that I'm somehow involved in whatever is going on?"

"Why do you think I'm pretending to be *your* husband, if you're not involved? Barry put you in the line of fire, would have taken you out himself if he wasn't so incompetent, no offense."

She stopped in her tracks. Blood drained from her face. No one had ever laid out what had happened in such a blunt way before.

"The one time his incompetence paid off, I might add," Sloan said. Something regretful crossed his face. Had it been when he realized his words had cut her to the quick?

He stepped toward her and she instantly backed away. The last thing she needed right now was sympathy in any form. She'd lose it if he touched her again.

"But why? Why did he want to kill me?" she asked, hating the way her voice quivered.

He looked at her bare legs for a moment too long then grabbed her hand and led her to the sofa. "Have a seat, I'll get the fire going before you turn completely blue."

"Aren't you going to answer my question?" Her ankle throbbed from overdoing it today.

"Take off your clothes," he said, ignoring her icy cold

glare.

"Like hell I will."

He grabbed a gray wool blanket off the back of the sofa and handed it to her. "Do it while I go collect wood for the fireplace to warm you up," he said. "You have to get out of those wet things." His expression turned into a warning. "Otherwise, I'll have to help you."

"You're not the least bit amusing." Images of him taking his clothes off the night before flooded her brain. Given his previous actions, she believed he'd carry out his threat. She quickly removed everything but her undies and jumped under the covers. The wool was itchy but warm.

Minutes later, he returned and dropped wood into the box next to the fireplace. He looked warm enough in jeans and a turtleneck sweater; whereas, she felt like a Popsicle. He barely acknowledged her until the fire was crackling happily and blazing enough to send out heat. When he stood, his moved slower than before. Probably had a few bruises after his fight with Preston.

"Better now?" he asked.

She nodded, although in the last few minutes her skin had begun to feel like it was on fire in places.

"Except you're not better, are you? What's wrong?" He frowned.

"I think it's the wool. It's really itchy," she said. She felt raw and extremely uncomfortable where the wool rested on her bare skin.

"So, take the blanket off. After all, it's not like you haven't seen me in my skivvies."

A hot flush bled up her neck. His comment wouldn't have been quite so bad if she hadn't already been visualizing him that way. "And, I'm sure you remember my reaction," she said. "So you know I'm not about to strip for you."

Humor flickered behind his eyes while his mouth

remained in a stern line. "Now you're making me feel like a male stripper."

She dug her nails into the side of her leg. Scratching just made the itch worse.

He adjusted the black turtleneck that cradled his face. Crazy, but she had a thing for that face, and, if not because he resembled Barry, then why?

"You can't stay under that blanket and scratch yourself raw. I'll get you some of my clothes to wear."

"No!" Wearing his clothes would be just too personal. Another wave of itchiness attacked.

"I'll be back in a sec."

When he returned he held a T-shirt in one hand and a pair of track pants. The shirt would easily go down to her knees. Since her skin felt raw wherever the blanket rubbed against it she decided to accept his offering. Her ankle was throbbing so she rested it on the arm of the sofa to elevate it.

Sloan looked at her foot sticking out from under the blanket and cursed softly. "That looks sore. I'll get some ice then I'll wrap it."

"The T-shirt first," she reminded him. He still had it clutched in his hand.

He held it just out of her reach. "Sure you wouldn't like to put it on now, before I go? Just in case you need some help." Her smiled at her.

"Not funny," she snapped, leaning over as far as she could without falling off the couch and grabbing the shirt from him. He actually laughed out loud as he turned and sauntered out of the room.

She straightened her shoulders, reminding herself he wouldn't let her off the island when she had the chance. He'd stopped her from getting away with Davey's friend. What a confused mess she was in. She also reminded herself that even though he'd saved her from Preston, he still had an agenda of his own and until she knew exactly what that was, she needed to stay on her guard.

She shoved the blanket off, pulled on his T-shirt and looked at the red rash over her legs. She was allergic to wool all right. In the crackling light of the fire, the rash looked nasty.

"Geez, your skin looks terrible," he said, returning a minute later with ice cubes wrapped in a tea towel for her ankle.

"Thanks a lot."

He handed her the cold compress. "This should help."

"What are you playing at? Bad crook, good crook?" she snipped. The burning, itching welts on her bare legs seemed to be her undoing. It was stupid to be undone by a rash in comparison to being kidnapped and targeted by killers, but it felt like the rash tipped the scales.

Smart enough to put some distance between them, Sloan sat at the other end of the sofa with his elbows on his knees and his hands clasped in front of him. A muscle worked in his jaw. Something was bothering him.

"What's going on, Barr... er, Sloan?" She waited for the worst news possible. The other men were back or something equally horrible?

"There's no other way to put this," he said. "I need your help." He got up briefly and poked the fire before he sat down again. The fire hissed and the flames licked higher inside the grate.

"Help you? How?" She pulled her feet underneath her.

He hesitated while obviously considering what he should tell her. That ticked her off. She wanted the whole, unvarnished truth—not pieces of the truth—and certainly not lies.

"Look, if you think I have any idea what Barry was up to, you're going to be sadly disappointed, because as far as I know, he had no ambition outside of selling his pots and pans."

"I can promise you he never sold a single pot."

Unable to sit still, she jumped up and tested her ankle then limped across the room and lowered herself onto a footstool near the fireplace. The crackling smokiness of the open grate and the extra heat blasting at her finally made her feel warm. She tugged Sloan's T-shirt down over her legs while she stared into the blaze and tried to make sense of everything.

Could it be true that Barry hadn't really sold pots and pans? She'd never seen him mention his wares to a soul. She'd never seen him sell anything. At the time, she thought it was because it wasn't professional to push himself at their limited circle of friends outside business hours. Once he'd even been asked about his product and he put the person off, saying he'd call them later. Now, she wondered if he ever did call them.

Before she lifted her head to Sloan, she said, "I can't help you even if you think I can. I don't know what Barry did when he was away on sales trips." She made a cynical noise. "Maybe he *was* hunting for treasure and that's why we pretty much lived on my salary, I just don't know."

"What I need to tell you has very little to do with your dead husband. It's about you, Raven Delacoeur."

She stared into his eyes. "Why am I not surprised you know my maiden name?"

"Your name is at the heart of everything that has happened to you, if you pardon the expression." He knew a little French, evidently. Her name meant 'of the heart'.

"You're saying my name was the reason Barry married me? Like I'm some movie star heiress with a name that opens doors?"

He nodded in agreement. "Yes."

"You're telling me that Barry met me on purpose that day at the grocery store and not by chance?"

He shrugged his shoulders. "I'm sorry, I know how

hard this must be to hear."

His words washed over her without much impact. She heard them, but they didn't register. "We bumped into each other at the cash register," she said, more for herself than for Sloan. She thought about that meeting. He'd bumped into her by mistake and caused her to drop the cans of tomatoes she'd been putting in her cart. He'd been very apologetic when he picked them up. After that, he helped her put the rest of the groceries on the conveyor belt then insisted on putting them in the car for her.

"He set me up," she said aloud.

Sloan's gaze averted. Had that been pain she'd seen in his expression?

* * * * *

Sloan cursed himself. How far should he go with the truth? Especially since she'd never been indoctrinated into her own family secrets.

Was she even strong enough to know the whole truth? She'd been through a lot, including traumatic amnesia as a teen. Not that he could tell her everything yet, damn it, because he didn't know everything himself.

"Why then? Why did he seek me out?" she asked. "What did he want from me?"

Sloan cleared his throat. "I'm sorry. I know how hard this is to hear. That doesn't mean he didn't love you in his own way."

"He tried to kill me!" she spat out. "I want the truth. It's not like I'll be broken-hearted to learn he didn't feel undying love for me. I already know that's not true."

Gritting his teeth, Sloan said, "Barry needed access to your belongings. He knew your parents died when you were a teen and I imagine he figured the information would be easier to locate if he was your husband. It probably put a crimp in his style when he found out you didn't know it existed."

"It?" She raised her eyebrows cynically. "I don't have anything of any value except a moldy old house filled with junk that belonged to my uncle and a lease on an apartment. If my family had something precious, don't you think they'd have told me? At the very least, they'd have mentioned it in their Will."

She had no reason to believe him and the truth sounded farfetched even to him. Too bad her family hadn't had the chance to tell Raven about her legacy. It would have been hard enough to believe coming from them.

"I'm not exactly sure what I'm looking for. What I do know is that it's key to finding something very valuable. It could be anything. I haven't been able to glean much from Brimm or his men in the last few weeks, but through discussions with Brimm, I did manage to eke out information that Barry believed it was here inside the house.

Sloan focused on the ocean view beyond the window. Initially, after Barry died and Sloan had met Brimm in person, he'd promised to have the artifact within six months. A year later, Brimm probably wasn't going to wait much longer.

"I've been trying to string them along in order to figure it out." He fidgeted with the tassel on the pillow beside him. "Even though I knew there was a hint of a chance you might be able to help me, I didn't want to involve you because of the danger element. But the truth is, you are involved now, and I need your help."

She crumpled just a little before taking a deep breath. "Crazy. This is just crazy. My family, we were just ordinary people who had no secrets or artifacts worth killing over."

No sense arguing with her—she was after all, missing crucial information.

"You really expect me to believe I've got something valuable enough that my life is in jeopardy over it? And my not-so-dearly departed husband tried to kill me over it?" She picked up a piece of bark that had fallen onto the hearth and tossed it into the flames. It lit on fire immediately and curled up into red-hot embers.

"Yes," he said solemnly.

"And, you don't think he found it?" she said tentatively. "Whatever it is?"

He shook his head. "According to Brimm, Barry hadn't found what he was looking for but he was supposed to be close." The last statement came out through gritted teeth. Damn it, he needed to find that artifact and fast. "He might've told Brimm that to save his ass, it's possible he had no clue where to look."

She closed her eyes and inhaled a little more raggedly than usual. She was obviously trying to keep her emotions in check. He wished she could let herself cry, or do whatever she needed to do since she'd been through hell the last few days.

It came as a surprise when his feelings for Raven hit him this hard again. He thought he was over her a long time ago and hated the gut-reaction he felt at that doe-in-the-headlights expression she'd been wearing since she'd arrived here. "So, did you find the boat today?"

"No."

He grabbed at a chance to change the subject. "Told you, you wouldn't find it."

She stood and turned her back to the fire. She was a vision in that T-shirt and those long, albeit slightly blotchy legs captured his attention for too long.

"I don't know how you hid the boat, but you did a good job," she said. "What do you plan to do with me now? You going to make me disappear too? Or are you going to continue holding me prisoner? Have you even considered that Burton might inform the police?"

"Who?"

"The guy in the rowboat."

"Oh, him." He still wanted to know where the guy had come from and how Raven had managed to find him to take her off the island. Whether she knew it or not, she acted like a Delacoeur. Resourceful. "Doesn't matter because we're leaving, probably today."

"Good, let's go."

Apparently she didn't care about the reasons. She just wanted to go home. She wanted to get away from him as soon as possible. His gut took a hit again and he ground his teeth together. "You surprise me, Raven. After all you've done to find the truth about Barry, could you leave now without knowing everything? Aren't you curious?"

"Not any more."

She was lying, he'd bet on it.

"I thought I wanted to know about Barry, but maybe I've changed my mind. Maybe I want out of here more," she said.

Sloan couldn't get the incident on the beach out of his mind. Yeah, she wanted off the island, but how'd she meet up with that guy? "How did you find the man in the boat?"

She stared at her hands. "He just happened by."

"Really? Just happened by? You could see him through all that fog?"

"Heard him actually," she said in a staccato voice that made it pretty obvious she was making it up as she went along. "I heard his boat engine."

"And you… what? Called out and he heard you over his motor?" He used his best you'd better talk cop-look, not that he'd ever been a cop, he'd just perfected the look.

She laughed, but it came out hollow. "Funny how fog carries things, isn't it?"

Yeah, like hell that's how it happened, but she wasn't going to tell him how she did it, not even if he begged. "I wish you could trust me, Raven."

"Trust you? I married a man who tried to kill me. How soon do you think trust will come again? Especially toward a man who kidnapped me and professes to want the same things my husband wanted?"

She had a point. And, she had every reason not to trust him, but he had to convince her otherwise and quickly. "I didn't want to tie you up but I didn't have time to wait until you came around in order to explain the situation to you. It was imperative that you were quiet and out of sight. My only option at the time."

Heat sparked behind her gaze. She had a temper when she wasn't scared out of her wits. Kitten had claws and she might need them to get out of this situation, especially if she got caught by one of Brimm's men.

"Oh, I'm sure you didn't want to keep me prisoner," she said in a caustic voice. "And, given the information about treasure, I bet keeping me here won't benefit you at all." She crossed her arms over her chest and dared him to say she was wrong.

He got up and approached her. Surely he'd proven himself trustworthy when he put his body between her and the gun. She had to know he wasn't a bad guy—right? Still, something akin to determination lit behind those beautiful blue eyes and he halted his progress. He couldn't even guess what she might be devising now, but whatever it was would probably surprise him, something like jumping out a two-story window into a slippery oak tree.

"Listen, I don't care what you're doing here, I just want my life back," she said.

"Really?" he said, fighting an urge to grab her shoulders and compel her to look at him. "Do you honestly expect me to believe you don't get a secret thrill from taking a risk? Aren't you dying to know what the hell is going on here? You might have been able to hide the truth from others, maybe even from yourself, but you can't fool me, you're a risk taker, Raven Gale. You wouldn't be here, otherwise."

Against his better judgment he took her hand in his and waited for her to freak out because he was touching her.

What had happened to the man with iron will and unfaltering control? He was on a steep, precipice right now and at risk of falling over. He ignored the warning sirens in his head while he deliberately trailed his fingers up her arm and caressed the side of her neck. It was a test—and she hadn't run away screaming.

This was wrong—she must have sensed his misgivings because her eyes narrowed on him and the cold hard truth dug into him. No matter how he felt about her, she'd never be able to care for him, especially when she learned the whole truth about his family.

He let go and she turned away to pick up her semi-dry clothes.

One thing he knew about Raven Delacoeur, she'd been hurt too many times to trust him, or anyone.

After everything he'd done to her since she arrived on the island, how could he expect her to trust him?

There was no doubt in his mind that she'd run the first chance she got. If only he could make her understand that he was on her side.

* * * * *

Raven bit her lip. If only she wasn't curious enough to want to move a fricking mountain to find out what was worth killing her to get. Damn it.

Right now she needed to focus on getting herself out of this mess. No way did she want to be drawn any further into such a dangerous situation. Her shoulders were stiff while she turned the damp clothes over on the hearth to dry.

"You might have been able to trust me if I'd had the

luxury of explaining the situation to you when you arrived. We might've even been friends," he said."

She readjusted her shirt on the stone hearth. How long could she stay squatted down here moving her clothes around so she wouldn't have to face facts? Sloan handsome and he'd pretended to save her, but could she trust what he'd done wasn't faked? No. His tricks wouldn't work on her. "That's really not very likely, is it?"

"Maybe not." Even so, he sounded hurt, and that didn't make sense.

She stood, tension building in her chest. "You kidnap women and hold them hostage, you can't expect any sort of normalcy after that."

Even though he nodded, he looked somehow hurt. "It was a bad start, that's for sure and I guess there's no way I can justify what I did. At least not right now."

She inched to the end of the sofa. "Oh there's a way you can prove it. Let me go. Get me off this island and on my way home."

His mouth tightened. "That would be one way to show my true intent."

There was a huge 'but' in his statement and she didn't like it one bit. She put her hands on her hips. "What other possibilities could there be?"

Was it possible his gaze compelled her to understand him, to give him a chance? Darned if she knew how he was doing it, but it was working—as much as she didn't want it to happen, there was chemistry between them. It was official, she'd lost her mind.

"One possibility would be for you to stay here and help me," he said.

"Are you totally delusional? Why would I ever consider doing that?"

"Because I'm being honest and asking for your help. I promise to keep you safe."

She sighed. "Yeah? Thanks, but no thanks. I want out of here." She started to leave the room, but paused and looked back at him. "Out of curiosity, what are your qualifications in the keeping me safe category?"

"Right now I'm a university professor," he said in a lowered voice.

She leaned against the door casing, her knees suddenly gelatinized. "Great. Doesn't sound like you're an expert at being a bodyguard, does it?"

"I was also in the military."

She remembered what he'd said in his sleep about everyone being dead. "Did you see action?"

A shadow crossed his face. "Yup."

Note-to-self, don't tell him he talked in his sleep. He'd probably freak if he knew she'd heard him talking.

"And now, you help criminals in your spare time?" She hoped he heard the disappointment in her voice.

"It's a long story."

She hiked an eyebrow.

"Raven?"

The way he'd just said her name made her heart flutter. He was doing that thing to her again, and she was helpless against it. She bit her lip.

Maybe weakness showed on her face because he suddenly stepped closer and took her in his arms. She didn't fight him. His mouth brushed hers, tentatively.

Okay, maybe she wondered what kissing him would be like, but she'd be darned if he'd get the reaction he expected. Only, at the moment while his mouth pressed against hers she wanted to melt into him. Oh God! He was good.

Given the adrenaline pumping in her veins, somehow she managed not to react. Not to kiss back.

He stopped. "I'm sorry Raven, that was inappropriate and I don't imagine it made you feel any safer around me."

He couldn't have been more accurate. Worse, the

unwanted and unwarranted attraction threatened the self-protective bubble she'd formed around herself. Did she need the cold hard truth to rear up and bite her, to remind her that he wasn't who he said he was? "You apologize for kissing me, but not for holding me prisoner?"

"I thought I'd already told you I was sorry about restraining you?"

She considered his words. "Maybe you did. Maybe I just didn't believe you."

"I guess I can't blame you for that." He looked at his watch. "At least I'm taking you off the island."

"I can't get out of here fast enough," she admitted, rushing to the hearth to gather her semi-dry clothes.

"Hold up," he said. "We'll go, but not until the tide comes in tomorrow morning. We'll get a good night's sleep tonight."

"Why the heck didn't you just say that," she said, dropping everything. She rocked back on her heels aware that he was staring at her and afraid the T-shirt might be see-through in front of the fireplace. She jumped up, crossed the room and curled into a wingchair near a window. Once she sat, she wished she'd stayed nearer the fire since it was cooler in this section of the room. Oh God, she had no clue what she was doing right now.

"Raven, we have to talk about something very important before you get back to the mainland," he said in a serious tone.

She frowned at him. Hadn't he already told her the worst?

He leaned against the fireplace mantle and stared into the flames below. "When Barry tried to kill you, he set a chain of events in motion, events that can't be stopped. He told secrets to the wrong people and they want a payday."

"What kind of secrets," she asked, steeling herself for his next bomb.

"It involves your family. There are things you don't know about them. Things they didn't have time to tell you."

"You're making this up."

"I'm not."

First, according to Sloan, her parents had some sort of key to a treasure and now there was some other deep, dark secret about them she supposedly didn't know.

"Your husband did something that's never been done before by a Protectorate member, not since their beginnings in the sixteenth century. Barry divulged secret information to outsiders. Secrets that aren't meant to get out."

"Protectorate member? What does that mean?"

"He, and your family were members of a secret society."

"You're lying."

"I'm not, it's the truth. Your parents were very important members of The Protectorate. They guarded certain ancient relics."

Her brain was about to explode. She jumped out of her chair and raised her hands into the air. "That is crazy."

She started pacing, every now and then stopping long enough to look at the ocean, her only escape from this madhouse. Finally she turned on him. "You say he divulged secret information. Aren't you doing the same thing right now by telling me?" she asked.

He shook his head. "No. And do you want to know why I'm not divulging information to an outsider?"

Did she want to hear this? She curled herself into the wing chair again.

"It's because you're not an outsider. You're a member by virtue of your birth. You're one of us."

Oh man! She sighed. Did he really think she'd swallow this stuff? "Why didn't Barry just ask me for whatever it is, if it was so valuable? I probably would have given it to him."

"He couldn't risk it. He desperately needed the artifact

in order to find the treasure. If you'd found out about your parents' history, you might not have been so willing to just give away their legacy without question. In fact, I'm sure of it."

"My parents' legacy?"

He nodded. "They were senior members of The Protectorate."

Something about those words niggled at her but she couldn't pin it down. She had the feeling it was true. Why couldn't she remember?

Next, she thought about the possibility that Barry had been trying to find treasure that her family protected. "Wait a minute, after my uncle died, Barry and I went to his house once. Barry looked through the place for me. He even went through the attic where my parents' belongings were stored after their death." She swallowed hard and turned away for a second to regain composure. "I didn't have the heart to go up there and look through their things. It just brought back memories best forgotten. If there was anything there, he most likely already found it."

Sloan had the decency to look sympathetic. "According to Jason Brimm, Barry didn't find anything at your uncle's place. Barry had a lot riding on getting that information and Brimm doesn't take no for an answer."

Her suspicions heightened. "I suppose you're thinking if Barry could play me for a fool, it'll be easy for you to do the same thing. Well, you can forget it, no one is going to use me ever again."

Sloan dropped his gaze to the floor. "Do you really think I'm anything like him?"

"The only thing I know about you is that you're an imposter and a kidnapper, how could I possibly know if you're like him or not?"

"I saved your life out there in the field," he reminded. "And, believe it or not, you're not being held against your will, merely being protected until I can get you to safety."

She spiked an angry glance in his direction. She was terrified, but too stubborn to let it show. "It's bad enough that my whole marriage was a sham, that my husband didn't love me and only wanted me for some artifact that was worth killing me to get, but now I've been kidnapped by you and you seem to think you can dupe me into helping you, too."

"I'm not that guy." His voice deepened and his fists clenched ever so slightly. "But, your family..."

"My family?" She cut him off in a caustic tone. "They're all dead, or didn't you notice when you were doing your research on me?"

"I know. I'm really sorry about that."

She looked away from him and bit back a retort. Darn him. Even worse—he did look sorry. "And just what is the truth about my family?"

"I know some of it, but not all. Finding the artifact will help you see with your own eyes what your parents really did for a living. I'm sure you won't believe me until then, but I can pretty much guarantee they wanted the same thing for you."

She stilled. What was he trying to say? That her parents were criminals like him? That was why they were always gallivanting around the globe? Not likely. Her parents were the most moral people she'd known. They'd never be like him. "You'll do anything to get what you want won't you?"

He rested his hand on the mantle and stared into the fire again. "I do want to discover the location of the artifact, but not at your expense, Raven, and certainly not at risk of your life. If we do this right, it'll benefit you more than anyone else. I'm not duping you. I'm trying to give you the information you need to stay safe. I certainly don't enjoy being the one to tell you about things your parents' would have told you themselves if they'd been alive to do it. They'd have wanted to initiate you into their world. With Brimm going after you, you need as much information as possible to arm yourself against him and others like him, especially now that word is out making the Protectorate a target for every criminal on the planet. Members of The Protectorate will be in constant danger, and so will you, by virtue of your heritage."

"I'm not a member of The Protectorate."

"You were born a member. Unfortunately, at this point, the criminals know more about it than you do. Barry sold us out, until he came along The Protectorate has always been a group whose members would rather die than give up their secrets."

"Do you expect me to believe there's no benefit to you if we find treasure?"

His shoulders bunched up around his ears. "Yeah, finding it'll benefit me too. But mostly you."

"Get me home and I'll consider what is true and what isn't," she said, thinking she'd dump him the first second she got.

"There might be an added bonus for you to find the whole truth," he said. "There are some things about your family even I can't tell you."

"Like what?"

He shrugged. "Like what they were protecting. No one knows and no one has been able to figure it out since they died."

She rubbed her temples. "Surely someone kept records?"

"No. Three top individuals held the locations of the treasures in their own way, but the locations are never recorded. And, because the Triumvirate in charge of The Protectorate at the time were killed shortly before your parents, the location of your parents' treasure was lost."

She chewed on the edge of her lip the whole time she

listened to him.

"See what I mean? There are things you should know. If you stick with me for a while, you'll find the answers to those questions. Your parents spent their whole married lives protecting this treasure, surely you don't want someone else to get their hands on it?"

"I don't know what to think. How do I know my parents really did these things? How do you know they did?"

"My family belonged to The Protectorate, too." He stared out the window just as the room brightened a little when the sun made an attempt to break through the thick curtain of fog.

"Looks like the weather might be improving," she said vaguely then switched her attention back to him again. "And Barry? Will I find some answers about him, too?"

Sloan stared at the warm brown hardwood floor. "He didn't deserve you."

"Sorry?"

"He was a son-of-a-bitch," Sloan said and cursed himself for his thoughtlessness the second her eyes closed. She had been married to the idiot, after all. She must've had some feelings for him. And now he'd insulted her choice of a husband. "Look, I'm sorry, I had no right to…"

She straightened her back and spread her shoulders. "No. You're right about him."

"It's not fair to talk about him now that he's…" Oh God, he was really putting his foot in it today. Good going, Brockway. Remind her that her husband's dead. Real smooth.

"Dead?" She crossed her arms under her full breasts reminded him she had nothing on but filmy undies and his T-shirt. He swallowed hard. Damn it. He knew how to disassociate his feelings, so why wasn't he this time?

"You mentioned earlier that you were at Barry's funeral?"

At least she hadn't noticed him ogling her. He tried to focus on her question but she looked like a little bit of heaven in that T-shirt with her blonde hair curling over her shoulders.

"Mmm hmmm."

"You saw his body, then?" she asked.

That question broke into his impure thoughts. "No. It was a closed casket," he said slowly, quietly, trying to create a calm demeanor to help soothe his unbidden desires.

"Who asked for a closed casket?"

Sloan thought for a moment. "It wasn't you?"

She looked like she was bracing for a revelation she didn't want to hear. "Maybe Barry had made arrangements with his lawyer in case anything happened to him? It might have been a final request?" Sloan asked.

With a shake of the head, she said, "No. As far as I know, he didn't have a lawyer. *We* didn't have a lawyer until I hired one after Barry died to handle the paperwork. Since I was hospitalized after the accident and there were no other relatives, I've been trying to find out who handled the burial. When I questioned the mortician, he said a friend of the family who wished to remain anonymous, attended to the funeral costs. Apparently, they had a note with Barry's final wishes written on it."

Sloan frowned. "Have you still got the message?"

"No, the funeral home threw it away before I could see it."

"Convenient," he said quickly then thought about how his words might upset her. "Raven, I..."

She held up a hand. "Doesn't matter. None of it." Her body language told a different story. It did matter.

"You must've been surprised when you got out of the hospital to find out Barry had already been buried."

She nodded but didn't look at him. "That's to put it mildly. I was not only surprised but angry, I needed the closure his funeral would have afforded me."

He rubbed his hands together over the fire.

"I did finally manage to get a copy of the coroner's report. Barry's upper body had apparently gone through the windshield. But where did the note come from? And who handled the funeral arrangements without consulting me?"

"I don't know the answer to that," he said. "It's been over a year since the funeral, whatever made you come to this island looking for him now—you knew he was dead?"

"Because of the way the funeral was handled, I had a niggling idea that Barry wasn't really dead. A short while ago, I decided to finally get rid of his things." She shrugged. "Perversely I'd kept everything for reasons that I can't explain. I should have tossed his belongings lock-stock-and-barrel right after the funeral. I was preparing his clothes and other items for Goodwill when I found a map in his briefcase along with papers and invoices for ferries on the east coast. I immediately went out and hired a detective who traced Barry's travels the last few months before his death. Hartt Island was one of his most often visited destinations. That's why I came here, that and the fact that someone using his name lived here—I half expected to find him alive."

Sloan exhaled heavily. "We both saw the grave."

"But what if it wasn't Barry inside that coffin?"

"I'm sorry?"

"What if he *is still* alive?"

"Surely you don't think that even now, do you?" he asked, hating the way that thought obviously disturbed her. She needed to know Barry was truly dead because she was afraid of him. She wanted Barry gone and he didn't blame her.

Sloan would like nothing better than to be able to prove to her that her bastard, dead husband was in the grave in Chicago. Worse, he ached to make things better for her.

He wanted to lift her face to his, to taste those moist lips again, but she didn't remember him.

He clenched his fists into tight balls. For her sake, he'd avoided her for years. He was no good for her and at this point if he resurrected too many of her blocked memories it could all come flooding back and God only knew what that would do to her.

As a distraction, he tossed another log on the fire and watched the sparks fly up the chimney. Maybe Raven subconsciously wanted Barry back? Some women still loved husbands who were abusers, but he couldn't imagine that she was one of them. "I'm sure he's gone, Raven. Nothing can bring him back."

"I don't think you understand how important it is for me to be sure," she said, moving around the room again, obviously unable to relax. "I want to make sure that bastard is dead."

He should've known she'd be too smart to be pining for that idiot.

"If you help me find the artifact, I'll help you prove he's dead, even if we have to exhume the body to do it."

She wrinkled her nose. "I hope it doesn't have to come to that."

"Will you agree to help me?" Sloan asked, he'd damned well make sure no one hurt her again, either. Not Jason Brimm, and not a dead man.

"I think I've proven I'm not a good judge of character. If I go along with you now, it doesn't mean I trust you."

"You can trust your instincts this time, Raven. As for Barry, he was a con man—you aren't the first person to fall victim to his cons."

She narrowed her gaze on Sloan, the man who looked so much like Barry and pushed her hair behind her perfectly shaped ears. Her eyes glistened a little too brightly.

Sloan ran a hand over his face. Barry had been in too deep with Jason Brimm long before he'd married Raven. His compulsion for treasure and gambling of every sort guaranteed that.

To make matters worse, Sloan had caught up with and confronted Barry the day before he tried to kill his beautiful wife. Never in his wildest dreams did he think Barry would attempt to hurt Raven, let alone kill her. No one saw that coming.

Now he had to find the very thing her parents had died to protect, and as much as he tried to convince himself he was doing this for her, finding the treasure would benefit him just as much. Maybe she was right. He was doing this for his own reasons.

CHAPTER SIX

WHEN THE tide came in the next morning, Sloan led the way to the boat, silently cursing himself. He'd bungled things royally with Raven. Of course, she was only being cooperative right now because he was taking her off the island.

Given the circumstances, he could have handled this whole thing better. For starters, making sure she had stayed in Chicago. True, no one could have guessed that she'd do something this out of character, but considering her family tree, he really should have realized it was a possibility, especially after she'd hired that private investigator.

Fog hung heavy around them again today, but as tiresome as it had become, it gave them cover. He glanced back at Raven once again dressed in her hearth-dried summer attire that wouldn't keep her warm for ten minutes out here. He'd tried, but couldn't convince her to wear some of his warmer clothes.

Her long hair spritzed with non-stop mist curled at the ends and bounced on her shoulders. She was still limping but keeping up with him without complaint. He had no idea where Brimm and his men had gone but he didn't discount the fact that they might still be around.

"This way," he said, leading her to the old stone out-building at the edge of the farm where they'd stashed Mike and Preston. He'd prepared enough food to hold them over until he returned or sent help. "You okay to walk a bit further?"

"I'm fine." She looked around. "Where are you taking me?"

"We have to check on our captives. I can't leave them without food and water if we're leaving the island. I'll call The Protectorate to come and get them after we hit the mainland. I managed to get out to feed Mike yesterday, but I haven't had time yet today."

"Oh!" she said. "I can't believe I'd forgotten about them."

He unlocked the door to the outbuilding on the edge of the field and entered while she waited outside. She probably had enough of captivity to last her a while. The musty interior of the decrepit building seemed worse in the foggy dampness, but it worked well as a holding cell with two high windows that allowed light to seep in on good days when the fog didn't block out the sunlight.

His eyes had to adjust to the dim light before he found Mike's shape in the bunk, still asleep. "Wake up you two."

He'd made them as comfortable as possible, too comfortable, maybe, because Mike was still asleep and covered head to toe. "Hey Cap, rise 'n shine."   Sloan reached out and poked the blanket. His hand sank into a straw mound under the covers.

A quick glance at the opposite wall where he'd left Preston made Sloan's hackles rise. They were both gone. They shouldn't have been able to get away on their own since they'd been manacled to iron rings nailed into the stone. He held up a manacle, it had been sawed off. Since there were no tools in the old shed alarm bells started ringing in his head.

Backing outside, he rushed toward Raven while keeping a sharp eye on their surroundings. "Bad news, the men are gone." He filled her in on the details. "I think we'd better head for the mainland, and the quicker the better."

* * * * *

Raven kept pace but kept glancing over her shoulder. She wondered about the old man named Davey? He'd seemed odd, maybe even senile. Was he still around? Had he been the one who'd released the men, and should she tell Sloan about him even though she'd promised she wouldn't?

Sloan stopped and she'd been so preoccupied with her thoughts she nearly ran into him. Her breath seized when she realized they were at the edge of a cliff, a very steep cliff that overlooked an angry-surf crashing viciously onto jagged rocks below. There was only one reason to bring her here. "You are going to kill me aren't you?"

"Definitely not. As odd as it seems, this is the only way to Mike's boat. Trust me."

He held out a hand and waited for her to come to him— to step up to the very brink of death. He could've just grabbed her and tossed her over if his agenda had truly been to kill her, but instead he waited.

She desperately wanted to go home and if this was the only way, what choice did she have? After a few baby steps forward, she looked down again and froze. It would be bad enough to fall to her death, but it'd be even worse to end up in that swirling ocean.

She shuddered.

If she followed him now it would truly be a leap of faith. Did she have that kind of faith in him? Or would she be proving her gullibility yet again, only this time at the cost of her life.

"What are you planning to do, fly to the boat?" she asked, realizing that her breathing was a little hard to get under control right now.

His gaze connected with hers and his features softened. "I promise you, this is the way to the boat. Can't you trust me?"

"No reason to," she said, clenching her hands and taking two solid steps back.

"I'd like to get off the island before one of our missing prisoners finds us. Trust your instincts," he said.

She gritted her teeth. Instincts? Assuming they were in his favor—did she even have any instincts that worked? After all, she had married Barry. Tension tightened her neck muscles.

Below her, the waves crashing against the rocks continued to instill a tight sort of panic in her chest.

The fact that he waited for her to choose made her a little less reluctant. Sloan was a big man, obviously a strong man, if he wanted her over the side of that cliff he could toss her off and she wouldn't be able to stop him. Since he hadn't done that yet, dare she hope this really was the only way to the hidden boat?

Another deep breath steadied her nerves in order to meet his gaze. "I'm not a mountain climber and I definitely do not have the experience to scale down the side of this cliff."

"Not a problem, I'll help you," he said. "There are just a couple of tricky steps down, then we'll be okay."

Once she got over the lip of the cliff, she could see rudimentary stairs carved into the side of the rock. Stairs to nowhere, as far as she could tell, then pretty much a sheer drop down to jagged rocks buffeted by monster waves. Sweat broke out on her upper lip and nape of her neck, and she felt a little like she might throw up. Vertigo swelled up and she closed her eyes to try and stabilize that off-kilter feeling.

Sloan waited on the next step, giving her room to follow.

"I can't," she said.

"I know this is scary but anyone who can jump from the second story of a house to scale down a tree in the dripping fog can take a few steps down these stairs with my help."

He had a point. She'd flung herself out that window

because she had to. And she had to do this, too.

"If I fall, I'm taking you with me," she warned through her teeth before accepting his hand. Hopefully, he couldn't feel her quaking inside.

When she lost her footing on the wet stone and slid the final few inches into his arms, she'd nearly panicked.

"You're okay," he said, quickly snagging her close to him and allowing her to grab the rock again.

She could feel his heart beating against her chest. Or was that her heartbeat? "I could've been smashed onto those rocks," she said in a shaking voice.

"But you weren't. I caught you."

"Thank you." It came out in a whisper, but he heard her and gave her a gentle squeeze.

"Ready to continue?"

She nodded. Not because she was hanging off the side of a cliff with a man who'd kidnapped her and who could just as easily toss her off and be done with her, but because his arm wrapped around her and held her firm. He'd kept her safe again.

No one had done that for her in a very long time.

On the other hand, this wasn't the time to let her sanity go, either. She couldn't let herself trust him or anyone else until she found out exactly what was going on.

"Ready to continue?"

"I'd say let go of me and I'll follow you, but I don't think that'd be such a good idea right now," she said, more terrified than irritated. "Don't let go of me, okay?"

"Okay. You'll be safe in a second. Crawl into that opening right there." He held her hand and led her down two more steps until the partially covered opening came into view.

It disturbed her that there was something about this whole scenario that sent her blood racing in her veins and not just in a scared-to-death kind of way, but a feeling alive for the first time in a very long time kind of way. How had Sloan been so right about her when she didn't even know it herself, until now.

She crawled on her hands and knees for about two feet then walked another couple of feet until she came to a ledge inside the cave. Below her, an inlet along with a natural docking bay complete with a wooden dock, and— she squinted in the darkness—Captain Mike's boat.

Coming up behind her and brushing dirt off his hands and jeans, Sloan reached over and flipped a light switch. "This place is huge, isn't it?"

She nodded agreement. "How many caves like this are on the island?" she asked.

"As far as I can tell it's riddled with caves, but most of them are virtually inaccessible. I've found a few of them, but not all."

This cave didn't look like a new discovery. In fact, it looked like it had been used for a very long time right down to having electrical wires, albeit ancient looking ones, in the walls where antique lights hung around the circumference of the place.

"Is there an elevator around here?" It was a long drop down to the dock. The only way down appeared to be via an old wooden ladder leaning against the ledge.

"Just the ladder I'm afraid."

"We're not going down on that?" It looked hand carved. How safe could it be?

He grinned. "Compared to scaling the slippery cliff outside, it'll be a piece of cake. It's quite safe, I assure you."

Sloan went first, and when she finally stepped off the last rung, she breathed a sigh of relief and felt her knees threaten to buckle. "No wonder I couldn't find the boat."

"I did try to tell you it would be impossible to find," he said.

"You didn't tell me why I wouldn't find it."

"Couldn't. This is a secret mooring site. Few people know of its existence."

"I know where it is now," she reminded.

"Yes, you do." He started toward the boat on the floating dock.

"How'd *you* find this place? It looks like it has been in use for centuries." The ladder alone looked like it was a hundred years old.

"I imagine it was used by rum runners in the prohibition." He scanned the natural formation. "I found the location on an old map."

"Is that how you found the house, too? Or do you own it?"

Sloan's attention immediately slid to her. Worse, he suddenly looked concerned.

"No, actually you do, Raven."

Her mouth seemed to be continually hanging open around this man. "Me? What are you talking about?

"I told you there were more things you needed to know."

"But, that can't be true. My solicitor would have told me."

"He most likely didn't know about this piece of property. Your uncle probably had the deed hidden someplace safe, we just have to find it to prove it to you."

Again he mentioned her uncle. "You know about my uncle, too?" He had died a few months after she married Barry. Uncle Phil been her last living relative and she missed him terribly.

Sloan shrugged his shoulders in a noncommittal way.

"How could that house be mine, I've never seen it before. I've never been here before."

He ignored her.

Ticked, Raven walked toward Captain Mike's boat and started to climb aboard. She just wanted to go home. She could do her own research when she got there, she didn't need Sloan. She didn't even know if he was telling her the truth.

"Let's take mine, it's faster," he said, touching the small of her back before she got to the top of the ladder on Mike's boat. He then pointed to a sleek, long-lined black and silver speedboat on the other side of the cavern.

They walked around the cave and boarded the boat that looked more his style than the bulky charter-boat belonging to Mike.

He indicated the seat next to his and waited for her to sit before he pressed a button to start the inboard motors, they purred like a lion while the vessel moved smoothly through the cavern opening, out to the open sea. When she looked back at the ragged cliff-face, the cave opening blended in so well with the jutting rocks it had disappeared. If she hadn't just exited that cave she'd find it hard to believe it existed.

"Can you maneuver safely in this fog?" she asked.

He pointed to the high-tech equipment on the dash. "I have all the gear." He eased down on the throttle until they were clear of some jagged rocks then throttled up again. Now they cautiously skimmed over the crests of the waves.

It felt eerie to be moving through fog this thick—eerie and dangerous, and somehow familiar. Raven began to feel as if she couldn't breathe. Her chest tightened to the point of near panic. What was wrong with her, lately? Her emotions were all over the place and sometimes it seemed she was reacting to things she'd experienced before but of course that was impossible.

They moved through the grey mass at a steady but safe speed. She wiped her face off several times, it felt like someone had thrown a bucket of water on her. Sloan had given her a lifejacket to wear over her own clothes but she was freezing. She shivered and tried to ignore the bone numbing cold. She'd even take that woolen blanket right now, rash or not.

A foghorn blew somewhere nearby. It sounded close. "Are we near land?" The sooner they reached the mainland and got into a coffee shop to warm up, the better.

"There's an archipelago of islands out here called The Wolves. Don't worry, my radar is good, but it's best to take our time and make sure we avoid any unexpected land masses."

"Good idea." She barely got the words out when the bow of another ship slid out of the fog like a spectral thing and rammed them. Their boat lurched sideways. She probably would've been knocked out if she hadn't been strapped into her seat.

"That idiot rammed us on purpose," Sloan said, yanking the wheel sideways to maneuver out of the impact zone. "Maybe he couldn't see us. Ahoy, there!"

After the impact the boat that hit them reversed engines and disappeared into the fog again. But it was still there, lurking just out of sight. They could still hear the engines running not far away.

Sloan checked his own craft over then focused on making headway through the fog and out of the path of the boat that had hit them. Fog had a way of making sounds do strange things. They hadn't even heard the yacht approaching, but now they could hear the distant purring of its engine, trolling along, either searching for them or following them.

"That wasn't a mistake, they're going to sink us, aren't they?" she said.

"Not if I can help it," Sloan ground out, his expression terse and determined. "Make sure your life vest has an EPIRB attached just in case."

"A what?"

"See that orange cylinder in the box beside your seat? Clip it onto your vest. It'll notify the coastguard if we capsize. You just have to push this button to arm it."

Raven picked the EPIRB up and clipped it onto her shirt then looked into the box for another one. "This is the only one? What about you?"

"I'm staying with you no matter what happens. Besides," he stole a quick glance in her direction. "I'm going to make sure neither of us needs to use that device, I have no desire to experience hypothermia today. At least I'm going to do my damned best to avoid those bastards next time."

Zing! Something whizzed past her head and slammed into the dash, splintering the polished wood as it went. "What was that?"

Sloan dove toward her, wrapped her in his arms while he unclipped her belt and slid her down to the deck. "Bullet! Stay down and for heaven's sake keep your head down."

After making sure she was safely situated, he reached up and gripped the steering wheel and throttled up, all the while scanning for the boat that was still hunting for them in the fog, waiting to attack them again.

There was no question in Sloan's mind, it was Brimm hunting them. He would, no doubt, expect them to make a run for it in the speedboat, but Sloan had a better idea. They weren't far from the Wolves now. He knew he might be able to hide out in a cove until they were safe. If they could get some land between them and Brimm, they could hide in a cove. That might give them a chance. If not, they were sitting ducks.

Brimm had much superior tracking equipment in his million-dollar yacht, he'd be able to play cat and mouse without any problems.

Suddenly all was silent around them except for the sounds of the ocean lapping at the boat, and that mournful foghorn.

"Did he leave?"

"Shh," Sloan said. "Old sailors trick. They've cut their engines and they're listening for us. He geared down on the inboards so they were barely audible above the sounds of the ocean, and he slowly, quietly motored toward The Wolves so they could disappear.

Sloan suspected Brimm had only rammed them to scare them. He was playing with them. At this point, it'd be better to put some distance between them so he revved the inboards regardless of the noise and aimed for The Wolves where coves and inlets dipped in and out like puzzle pieces. Once inside the first cove, he throttled back and idled along quietly. He thought he'd lost them until the sound of a bullet whizzed past his left ear, slamming into the side of the boat.

"Stay down," he shouted and gunned the engines hard. They sped off. The yacht was close enough behind them to see it through the fog.

Another bullet zinged past. He'd have to risk it; he jumped back into the seat aiming for another island, and then another, circling several small islands with Brimm hot on his wake.

Sloan sped up on a stretch of water that he knew well enough not to sink them in these treacherous waters. Brimm's captain wasn't quick enough, or didn't know this area as well. They slowed and fell behind. It was long enough to enable Sloan to duck into an island cove and nestle the boat up against the shoreline. This time Sloan took a huge chance and cut the engines.

"There's enough shrub growth here that we should be able to blend into the background so they can't find us," he whispered.

They both heard the yacht motor trolling by. They even saw the shadow of its hulking shape in the fog like something spectral just off the shoreline. Its motors were reverberating at very low rpms as it moved by then disappeared.

"I think the Bay of Fundy's famous thick fog just saved us."

"And my superior boatmanship," Sloan said smiling, but it wasn't a true smile.

He was probably just trying to ease her worries, but she was well aware that his attention remained focused on their surroundings in case Brimm returned.

After another half hour that felt more like forever, Sloan seemed to relax a little. They'd waited virtually unmoving and listening for any indication that Brimm had returned. The good news was they hadn't heard his engines for quite a while.

Raven shivered on her seat and wondered if she'd be able to move when she got out of the boat. Her bones felt like they'd fused together from the cold.

"I think we can make a break for it. We need to reach the mainland before the fog lifts." He glanced at his watch. "That'll happen when the tide turns and then we'll lose our cover.

Following his lead, she crawled back into her own seat at the front of the boat. It was getting way to easy to allow him to protect her and he was right about the fog, it didn't seem quite as heavy any more.

Suddenly she noticed a growing blot of red seeping into Sloan's shirt. "Oh my Lord, you've been shot."

He tugged his sleeve up and looked at his upper arm as if it were news to him. "The bullet just grazed me. I was lucky."

"Should we use a tourniquet?" She started to unbuckle the cloth belt on her waist.

He laughed low in his throat. "I'm not bleeding hard enough for that, Raven. They didn't nick an artery or anything."

"My parents wanted me to be trained to do just about everything," she said. "If I'd done what I was supposed to do, I'd be a crack shot right now. But after they died, even though they'd made training a codicil in their will, I wouldn't do it."

"You seem to have innate talents, though."

"It was almost as if they knew they were going to die and they wanted to make sure I learned everything I could to keep myself safe," she said, then made an exasperated noise. "And all I did was crawl into my shell and hide until I found a husband who didn't love me and wanted to kill me. If they could see me right now, they'd be so proud

"Don't do that to yourself, Raven. You are much stronger than you believe. I understand you reacted quickly during the car accident and it probably saved your life."

Her heart turned to lead. "And it killed Barry."

"You had no choice, it was you or Barry, after he aimed your side of the car at the telephone pole. Grabbing that wheel saved your life."

She shuddered. "I really don't remember much after that until I woke up in the hospital. Then to add to my stupidity, I come to this island and walk right up to your door to demand answers."

"Don't do this to yourself, "he said.

"I should've been tougher. Smarter. I should've been the person my parents wanted me to be, not some scared mouse hiding in the corner."

"Your parents would have been proud of what you did on that island. It took guts, and in the end you did everything right in order to survive."

"Think so?" She lowered her lids and wouldn't look at him.

"I know so." He stared off into the fog. "I'm surprised Brimm used the tactics he did. Pretending to leave the island then waiting off shore knowing we'd make a run for it once we found our prisoners missing."

"But you said you were the only one who could find

what they wanted? Why would they want you dead, too?"

"They must've figured out I'm not really Barry. I don't think they want us dead, though, if they did, we would be." He frowned.

"I finally grow a backbone, and I'm going to get us both killed," she said.

Sloan smiled. "Not going to happen. Besides, this isn't the time for you to go back into your shell. That's no way to live. Not for people like us." He reached out and squeezed her hand.

"There you go talking about me like you have an inside track, yet we've never met before." Her expression shifted to quizzical.

Suddenly, his heart leapt. Did she remember him? In a way, he wanted her to but it'd be better if she didn't. He didn't want to have to tell her that he was related, not only to the man who killed her parents and who single-handedly obliterated her life, but he and Barry were first cousins, that's why they looked alike. The truth left a bitter tang on his tongue.

"Sit back and relax if you can, we should be able to make the mainland before all the fog is gone."

"What if they're waiting for us there?"

He narrowed his gaze on the ocean ahead. "Then we'll do what we have to do to keep you safe."

CHAPTER SEVEN

RAVEN WATCHED the dark landmass of Grand Manan Island growing closer. Her insides felt jumpy and she wondered if they'd really make it ashore before Brimm showed up.

So far, so good—it seemed impossible but they were motoring up to Grand Manan without another vessel in sight. Instead of finding a dock, Sloan ran his beautiful speedboat right up onto the beach.

"You'll damage your boat!" she said, grabbing the dash.

"It shouldn't do any damage, besides, I want to get you inland as quickly as possible before any more surprises show up." He scanned the ocean while he tied his boat to a large boulder then pointed to a rough path for them to take off the beach.

The sun broke through while they threaded their way along the narrow path, it felt like an omen of good things to come.

"I think we should go this way," he said pointing to the right. "We don't want to be spotted from the beach, and so far our path is perpendicular to the water."

Making their way through thick blackberry brambles spiked another sense of déjà vu. Blackberries were her favorite. Bees buzzed around the plants and dew hung on the berries in glistening globes alongside spider webs that were illuminated by artistic drops of dew. The air smelled earthy and salty. She plucked one lush blackberry and popped it into her mouth. Flavor burst on her tongue instigating sudden unconnected images. Her parents? Blackberry dumpling? Something else beyond reach?

"I don't know what you plan to do next, but I'm begging you to please take me to the ferry. I want to go home," she said.

Sloan's mouth tightened. "Please trust me. I'll keep you safe."

"I think you've done quite enough. Besides, you need to get to the hospital to have your arm seen to."

"If I were really a bad guy, why would I keep you safe from Brimm and his men?"

"Probably because according to you, I've got something everyone wants. Something my own husband was willing to dupe me to get and when he couldn't find it, he was willing to kill me to get me out of the way. And now you want the same thing."

There was no sense trying to read his expression before she turned and scurried up the last few feet of the bank toward the sound of an approaching vehicle. A road had to be nearby. It had been an emotional day and it had taken a toll on her. "Do I have to die for you to get what you want, too?" she asked when he caught up to her.

"Of course not!" He stopped and propped a foot on a tree stump tie his sneaker. When he straightened, he pushed his sleeve up and looked at his bullet crease. "If I wanted you dead I could have let Brimm do it, couldn't I?"

"But then he'd know you weren't Barry for sure because I would have told him."

Sloan sighed. "True. But that's beside the point."

"Wouldn't you have been in danger, too?"

"Definitely. I won't lie—that had been part of my consideration when I tied you up and hid you in the house, but first and foremost I wanted to keep you alive."

"So you could get the artifact."

He slapped his forehead. "Damn it woman, you're hard to convince."

She looked repentant, but he didn't buy it. "I guess you have very good reason to be suspicious and I commend you for your survival instincts. And, yes, I want the artifact. Unfortunately Barry spilled too much information. If we don't come up with something, you'll find yourself in a much worse situation."

She started walking. "Is that a threat?"

He stalked behind her. "No. It's Brimm you'll have to fear, not me. Even though you don't believe me, we need to find out why the hell Brimm wants you dead. I don't understand that part. It seems to me you'd be more valuable alive. After all, who'd be better able to help find it?"

She shot him an angry look at him. "Says the man whose only concern is my well being. Hah."

"If I can't convince you to believe in me, I don't know how I can possibly protect you when you get back to Chicago."

"I don't need you or anyone else to protect me because I'm going to the police."

He grimaced. "In that case, you'd better find the right cop, one who isn't part of Brimm's underworld payola system. There aren't very many of them who are dirty, but it's a crapshoot. You might find the wrong one."

She clutched her chest dramatically. "You mean I have no one to trust but you? Dear me. Whatever will I do?" She ended the sentence with a black look just as a car came along. She stuck out her thumb but the driver ogled her and kept going. "Rude."

Sloan touched her arm. "Look, whether you want to help or not, I have to find that damnable artifact before this thing can be over for either of us. To do that, I need to get back to Chicago where Barry found something that lead him to that house. If I can recreate his steps, I might be able to find the clue. You sure you won't help me find it?"

A shiver tingled up her neck. "Nope."

"Not even if I can prove how your parents really died?

I can certainly prove that island and that house belongs to you. Won't that mean something if I show you I'm telling you the truth?"

She hesitated. "Maybe. But I want to go home first, then I'll consider looking at your proof," she said. Not really! She'd go to the cops and have his butt thrown in jail.

"I hope you're going to let me protect you until this is over," he said.

She glanced at his left bicep. The wound still oozed a little blood and his arm had turned several colors around the injury. It was going to be a monster bruise. "That looks really sore. Don't you think you should get stitches?"

He looked down at his arm and shrugged. "It's only a flesh wound."

"I bet you've been waiting your whole life to say that," she said, biting back an honest-to-goodness-smile.

"What's your answer, Raven? Do we stay together and figure this thing out?"

"You'll get my answer when I get home."

He looked at her with a gut-wrenching smile that thrilled and scared her at the same time. "Okay, at least that's a start."

* * * * *

Back in Chicago, they made their way through the airport's automatic doors where he attempted to whisk her inside a black sedan parked at the curb.

She'd considered shouting for help inside the airport but changed her mind. He might be lying about the cops, but maybe he was telling the truth and she'd be putting herself in more danger.

A man leaning against a black vehicle straightened the minute he saw them. He could be another thug for all she knew. He had the same broad shoulders, same stance with a telling bulge under his jacket. She glanced around looking for a security guard, but saw none. It was too late to scream now.

Was it really a gun? She's seen enough movies to know where people holstered their weapons and wore them under their jacket.

How had her life turned into a spy novel?

In hindsight, she should have taken those self-defense lessons but she'd been lost and grieving after losing her parents. Poor Uncle Phil had tried to fill the role of both parents for an angry, upset teen that wouldn't cooperate. She'd always adored Phil and hoped he understood why she'd been so difficult. She missed him so much!

"Johnson." Sloan said, "Meet Raven Gale."

"Mrs. Gale," he said in a monotone voice. "Nice to meet you."

Raven cast him a suspicious look and didn't respond.

"Let's get Mrs. Gale out of here, Johnson."

"It's Delacoeur. I'm having my last name changed the first chance I get," she said.

One of Sloan's eyebrows slanted up, quickly becoming his trademark ironic look.

He hustled her inside the car and climbed in beside her. The man named Johnson got in the driver's seat and pulled the vehicle onto the street.

"Where are you taking me?" she asked.

Johnson looked at Sloan in the rearview mirror as if he was wondering the same thing.

"To Mrs. Gale's apartment, Johnson." Sloan's mouth seemed permanently set into a grim line, she wondered if he ever relaxed and more importantly she wondered what he planned on doing after he got to her apartment?

Could she manage to fling the car door open and dive out of a moving vehicle? How many lives did she have left? By her count, she'd already used up a handful.

"Don't even think about it," Sloan said, as if he could read her mind. He met Johnson's gaze in the rear view mirror and gave a quick nod. Instantly, the doors locked.

Raven grabbed the door handle and tried desperately to open it.

"Why are you doing this? The minute you open the car door, I'm going to scream my head off." Why hadn't she done that in the airport when she had a chance?

Sloan's eyes were hard to read. His face had become a mask. "I just wish you didn't think the worst about me, Raven. I promise I'm not going to harm you. I'm doing my best to help you and though I know you'll be tempted to try to get away, bringing attention to yourself won't be ideal right now. Brimm has many connections in the city and he'll be looking for you."

Even though she knew it was a deliberate attempt to scare her and make her more willing to do whatever he wanted, a shiver skittered through her. There was always the chance Sloan was telling her the truth. If he really was being honest, where did that leave her?

"Don't be afraid, locking the car doors is merely a safety precaution since having you dive out of the vehicle into traffic wouldn't be a very good idea." His eyes flickered, but just for a second, then the mask was back. "Please try to relax."

* * * * *

Sloan rubbed the tight muscles in the back of his neck while Raven made an attempt to hide the fact that she was terrified. He'd tried to comfort her. Imagine that! As if he had the right to try to soothe anyone.

He forced his mind to go blank. A talent he'd learned in Special Forces.

"If you think I'm going to keep quiet, you're crazy," she said in a low, angry voice.

A weary breath escaped him and he looked out his window. "You know what? When we get to your place, be my guest, shout the street down. But, if you go to the police, you'll never learn the truth about why your parents and uncle died." Those words hung in the air between them.

"No matter how many times you say otherwise, my parents drowned in a boating accident." A strange feeling ballooned inside her chest over this discussion. "Wait, are you saying whatever is going on right now has a connection to my uncle's death, too?" She gripped the door handle until fingers turned white. "Spill it!"

A lopsided grin worked at the corner of his mouth. "How did I ever think you were too fragile to take this news?"

"Since you don't know anything about me, I can't imagine?" She caught Johnson's twinkling eyes in the rearview mirror and glared at him too.

Suppressing a doubtful expression that would make her even angrier, he said. "Okay, here's the truth. Your parents were murdered."

"Ridiculous. They were sailing and their boat tipped over. They drowned," she said.

"That was a convenient story for the media. In actuality, they died for their beliefs. For The Protectorate."

"My parents loved travel and adventure. Neither of them worked, they didn't have to."

He pulled a ring out of his pocket and slid it onto his finger. She followed his gaze to the gold signet ring that looked very much like the one her father wore. "Where did you get that ring?"

"This ring?" He held it up for closer inspection. "Does it look familiar to you? Your father had one exactly like it, didn't he?"

"Yes. Is that his ring?"

"No. It's mine."

"Why do you have the same ring as my father?"

"I once belonged to the Protectorate. No one can know about us, not the police, not the government, especially not Jason Brimm and his thugs. We're a secret group, and we guard our information zealously. Your parents were among the hierarchy of our group, that should mean something to you."

Raven turned away from him. She didn't believe a word of it. Staring out the window at the familiar scenery passing by calmed her nerves a little because they really were taking her home.

"Your parents had a very important job and they were the best in their field."

"Was it important enough to risk their own lives and leave me all alone?" How gullible did he think she was?

"That's a question only you can answer when you learn the whole truth."

All these years she'd blamed her parents' adventurous ways for leaving her alone. She'd hidden herself from the world and from anything remotely on-the-edge, to prove to herself she wasn't like them. It seemed she recently thrown herself into a viper's pit and it didn't scare her nearly as much as it should.

"How do you know I won't go straight to the police or the FBI? Maybe I'll promise not to tell so you'll leave me alone, then I'll do it anyway."

He leaned closer to her, his arm stretched across the back of her seat. Liquid brown eyes captured her gaze and held it. "You won't because you'd undo everything your parents died for if you tell anyone. Not only did they give their lives for this cause, but this lifestyle was their wish and their legacy to you. Only, they didn't live long enough to see their hopes and dreams come to fruition."

"If that's true why didn't my uncle tell me about any of this? Or didn't he know?"

"I'm guessing after what happened to your parents, it was safer for you not to know until you were older." He tapped his fingers on the back of the seat. "Your parents were high level protectors, guardians of very important secrets and valuables. Each family in The Protectorate has their own artifacts to guard. As I told you before, only the Triumvirate is privy to what each family is protecting. It's safer that way. Problem is, just before your parents were killed, the Triumvirate were hunted down one by one, tortured and killed. Only they held the knowledge of all the locations of the relics. Not one of them gave up any information, though. That meant whatever your parents were guarding was lost."

She wondered how long it had taken to come up with such a complicated story.

He cleared his throat. "While I was serving my country, Barry stole my notes. I'd been commissioned by The Protectorate to do research on your family in hopes that their lost treasures might be found again and protected." Sloan ran a hand over his chin, rasping against unshaven whiskers. "He married you shortly after that."

"Why?"

"Barry must have hoped he could find additional clues to wherever your parents kept the treasures they were sworn to protect. If not from you, then from your uncle."

"Are you saying Uncle Phil was involved in this Protectorate?"

Sloan nodded. "It's a family trust. An honor to be chosen to protect the treasures of our past and our present."

"Only Barry didn't want the information for your Protectorate. He wanted it for himself." Realization was beginning to set in. It started to make sense.

"Unfortunately, yes. When your parents died, it was imperative that those secrets be discovered and turned over to someone else within The Protectorate until you were

ready to take over—if you decided to, that is. Several
people tried to find the key to the relics and failed. Your
parents were very good at their job."

She found little solace in that. Did that mean she was
starting to believe him? Just a little?

"That's when the new Triumvirate found out I was
searching, too. They decided to let me try where others had
failed. When Brimm turned up with information he
shouldn't have and I had the right appearance to pretend to
be Barry, I was chosen by the Protectorate to become him.
They managed to keep Barry's death quiet. It never made
the news here in Chicago and I stepped in and became him
for all intents and purposes."

"Minus his wife," she said.

Sloan nodded.

"But didn't Barry's lawyer know about his death?"

Sloan slanted a quick assessing look her way. "He was
one of us—and since you were fairly reclusive, it was easy
to take over without tipping off Brimm."

Raven blinked back tears. After she lost her parents,
she'd hidden from the world. When she'd married Barry,
he'd taken her out of the country where she only knew a
few acquaintances besides the lady across the hall from her
apartment.

"After the funeral, the only person connected to
Brimm, who'd met Barry face-to-face, was killed in a street
brawl in Chicago. That gave The Protectorate the ability to
send me in," Sloan said.

"That's how you ended up on the island with Jason
Brimm?"

"Yes and no. I was searching the island because your
parents owned it. It seemed the logical place for them to
hide whatever they had for safekeeping. I didn't expect
Brimm and his thugs to show up. Apparently before Barry
died, he told them about the island and about the treasure."

"And I went there totally oblivious to the danger," she

said in a faint voice.

"Right into the middle of it," he said. "I didn't think they knew about you, since your name had never been mentioned. Barry had told them all about The Protectorate and about the treasures we guard, the bastard! I heard one of the men say that Brimm intends to hunt down Protectorate members and their treasures one by one and he doesn't intend to leave any witnesses."

It all seemed so crazy. But little bits of what he was telling her began to gel in her mind. Small things her parents had said that she didn't understand. The rings they all wore. The whispering and secret trips they made. Could it be true?

"In a previous life, Johnson and I were in the military together. I hired him to keep an eye on you while I tried to find the artifact. It was never my job to be your bodyguard, nor Johnson's, but I had the feeling you needed someone on your side. There were two Protectorate men who were supposed to be watching you, but they weren't much good. I didn't trust them."

"It sounds like fiction," she said.

"I know it's a lot to digest. Especially when you learn your parents were agents for a secret society like The Protectorate."

"I need time to think," she said. "Time to figure it all out. If you really want the best for me, please take me home and leave me alone for a while."

"I'm afraid we can't do that, Raven. Whether you want Johnson as a bodyguard or not, you're going to have him. Either you agree, and he stays close to keep your safe, or he'll follow you everywhere you go and stay in the background. It's up to you."

"I thought you weren't holding me prisoner any longer?"

He visibly cringed, but ignored her comment. "You

probably won't see me again after we get you home. Just Johnson."

Johnson had been silent the whole time they talked, but his shoulders stiffened. "I'll protect you, Mrs. Gale."

"No, you won't," she said. "I'm finished with both of you. I don't want your protection, and I don't ever want to see either of you again."

"I'm afraid you don't have the option of sending us away. The Protectorate has a vested interest in your well-being and there's no way they're going to risk losing you now that you know about them."

"Once again, I feel like someone's commodity."

He ignored her comment. "Most women in jeopardy prefer the protection of an expert."

"Contrary to your belief that I can't look after myself, I can." She planted her hands on the seat for support. "The only reason you got the upper hand on the island was because I was dehydrated and I fainted. If I hadn't passed out there would've been no way you'd have be able to tie me up."

With an eyebrow quirked, he said, "Really?"

His amused expression angered her. "Really."

"And your parents? You don't want to find the truth about them?"

"No."

"We'll leave you alone, then," Sloan lied. She'd never know Johnson was still there, unless she needed him.

She cast a suspicious glance at him. "You're both going to do what I say? Walk away and leave me alone?"

"If you don't want us, we're gone," he said. He hated lying to her.

"Why don't I believe that?"

The car pulled up to the curb and Johnson turned back to look at Sloan. "Sloan?"

"Do as the lady says, Johnson. She wants us to leave her alone."

Johnson nodded and the doors unlocked from the inside. Raven jumped out and rushed to the front of her building. She turned the key in her lock and looked back at them before stepping inside.

Her expression told Sloan everything he needed to know. She damned well knew she was in danger and she was afraid.

"Park the car here," Sloan ordered when they were safely out of sight. Johnson braked and pulled into a parking spot immediately. "Go back and keep an eye on Mrs. Delacoeur, but don't let her see you."

"What are you going to do, sir?"

"I've got a hunch I need to track down. Keep a very close eye on her Johnson, don't lose her. They'll be coming for her and, by God, you'd better protect her."

"You can count on me, Sloan.

He patted Johnson on the shoulder. They'd been through hell and back in the same military unit. Now that they were civvies, Sloan had hired him to help assist in his search. If he found the treasures, his family might again be trusted by the Protectorate. But first, he'd have to prove they weren't in collusion with Barry and Victor.

"Thank you, my friend," he said to Johnson and left on foot. He made it to the Brainerd Branch of the Chicago Library on 1350 W 89th St. in less than twenty minutes. According to the sign on the door, the two-story brick edifice remained open until 9 pm that night. He went directly to the main desk and asked for information on how to access their online databases. He knew that Barry Gale had spent many hours in the library in Toronto, Ontario in Canada where he'd taken Raven after they'd married. As far away from people she knew as possible. What better way to manipulate and control her?

After that, Barry had returned to Chicago for weeks at a time. Some of that time was spent in this library. But what had he found in the library that helped him in his search for the artifact?

Two hours later and no closer to finding anything cogent, Sloan closed the tome he'd been reviewing. If it had taken Barry weeks to find something to report to Jason Brimm, why should he expect to find the information any quicker? At least he had the option of asking Raven questions. Barry couldn't do that or his whole sham marriage would have fallen apart.

Rubbing a hand over his weary eyes, Sloan leaned both elbows onto the table. Why would Barry keep coming back to Chicago? Maybe he hadn't come to the library all that often? Maybe he went somewhere else, but where?

Tired, and without finding a single lead, he headed back to Raven's house to talk to Johnson. When he arrived, Johnson wasn't in the vehicle and even though he might be merely walking the perimeter, making sure his charge was safe, Sloan felt in his gut something was wrong. He zipped up his windbreaker and waited next to Johnson's vehicle for a moment. The hairs on the back of his neck were doing that thing they always did when something wasn't right. His men always swore he was psychic but he didn't believe in hocus-pocus. Nevertheless, he did rely on his gut instinct and it was screaming that something was wrong.

Raven's second floor apartment faced the street. Her lights were on. He'd feel better if he saw her moving inside. As if in answer to his wish, a shadow moved behind the living room curtains, only, there was no way that had been Raven. The body size and height was wrong.

Senses on alert, he slipped down the dark alley next to the building. He knew the codes for the security doors and slipped inside and moved up the stairs.

Where was Johnson? That hadn't been his silhouette in the window, either. That left only one other option and it wasn't good.

Reaching the second floor in double-time, his heart stalled at the sight of Raven's door being slightly ajar. He pushed the door open just wide enough to slip inside. There had been an obvious struggle inside, the floor lamp had been tipped over and the coffee table was on its side—splintered into two pieces.

He was just starting a room-by-room search when he heard a noise in the bedroom down a short hallway. Ready for the worst, he slammed his foot against the bedroom door and sent it flying inward. The doorknob crashed through the wall behind it and stayed there.

Raven jumped off the bed with a golf club in her hands. Johnson lay on the bed, his face ashen with dark red blood wicking across the front of his shirt.

"What happened?" Sloan shouted, quickly checking the perimeter of the room.

Johnson tried to get up but fell back with a grunt. "Sorry, Sloan, there were two of them. Shot me with a silencer then brought me in here to show Mrs. Gale what they'd do to her next if she didn't talk." He coughed and a little bit of bloody spittle covered his hand.

Sloan looked over his shoulder. "Where'd they go? It doesn't make sense that they'd just leave."

"Someone alerted them that you were coming into the building and they took off." Johnson looked suddenly grateful. "They thought you might have brought back up."

"Good thing Brimm sent idiots—I'll do a quick check of the premises," he said. "Be right back."

He strode through Raven's apartment checking the place, making sure it was all clear before he returned to his wounded partner. "You're going to be okay, Johnson. He checked inside his partner's shirt to see the bullet wound. "Can you get me some towels, Raven?"

She jumped up and ran down the hall, returning quickly with thick towels.

Why the hell was she still here? Why hadn't they at least tried to kidnap her? Maybe they didn't want her dead after all? Something about that had always seemed a little off. Now it was rotten.

"They burst in and got the jump on me. I didn't have time to react, before…"Johnson coughed again.

"Don't talk, partner. The bullet has punctured your lung." Sloan assessed the entry wound and started to yank his cell phone out of his pocket. "Did anyone call nine-one-one?"

Raven nodded vigorously, her eyes round and moist. "They should be here soon."

"Good. Before they get here, Johnson needs some preliminary care. Help me sit him up."

Johnson's head flopped forward, his breathing labored while they positioned him against the headboard of Raven's bed.

Little air bubbles were forming in the blood. "I need some scissors, tape and piece of plastic – clean as possible. Some sort of plastic wrap or a bag will do."

She disappeared into the kitchen and he could hear her rummaging through the drawers to get the necessary tools. While she did that, he checked Johnson's back. The bullet had gone all the way through.

When she returned, he cut a square of plastic and placed it over the bullet wounds and taped it around the outside. The plastic moved in and out when Johnson breathed.

"What does that do?" Raven asked.

He was losing air from his lung. I sealed the wounds to keep air in until the EMTs arrive to stabilize him." Sirens sounded in the distance, a very welcome sound.

"Will he be okay?" she asked.

"He's tough. He's been through a lot worse, haven't you, partner?" He touched Johnson's shoulder.

Sirens wailed outside the building now. "Hang in

there, the EMTs are here."

Within minutes the rattle of a gurney in the hall alerted them to the EMT's arrival. Raven ushered them into the room.

"Who did the first aid?" one of them asked.

"I did," Sloan replied.

"Good job."

"Unfortunately, got some practice in the Gulf."

The EMT nodded and continued to work on Johnson. They transferred him to a stretcher with the back up and moved him out of the apartment quickly. "We called the police, they're tied up with a major accident on the freeway so they'll meet you at the hospital."

Sloan's shoulders tightened. Great!

Seconds after the EMTs left the apartment Sloan grabbed Raven's hand. "C'mon, let's go."

"Go where?"

"To the hospital. I have to make sure Johnson is okay."

* * * * *

Raven wanted to hole-up inside her place and pretend none of this happened. "You don't need me to go, surely?" As worried as she was about Johnson, being at the hospital set her on edge. She'd spent the last several years of her life avoiding stressful situations, at least until she'd tracked Sloan down.

"I'm not leaving you here alone, not after whatever happened. Plus, I need you to fill me in on what went down."

He grabbed a coat off a hook by the front door and handed it to her.

The ambulance had already taken off around the corner on its way to the hospital when they reached the car and jumped in.

She thought about how calm Sloan had sounded when he reassured Johnson. But she saw the worry in his expression now. "He's going to be okay, right?"

"Sure he is. He's tough," Sloan said in an automatic response that didn't exactly mirror his facial expression.

They caught up to the ambulance and stayed behind it. "We're almost there," Sloan said, effectively changing lanes behind the vehicle.

"I'm not sure why I let you talk me into coming—I don't like hospitals," Raven said.

"Who does?"

"I never go to hospitals, though," she said.

His hands gripped the steering wheel tighter. "Why *did* you come, then?"

She thought about it. She couldn't say he'd strong-armed her, because he hadn't. All he did was hand her a coat. "I'm not really sure. I guess I feel I owe this to Johnson."

"What happened back there, anyway? Brimm's man found you and Johnson got shot protecting you?"

"Something like that," she said. "I'm beginning to believe you, if it's any consolation. They tried to shoot me but Johnson managed to stop them by jumping in front of me. I think he managed to wing one of them in the process."

"Was it Brimm himself?" Sloan asked then realized she hadn't seen him. "He's overweight, balding and wears heavy gold bracelets?"

"No. One tall, thin man and the other one was tattooed and looked like a biker. I saw one of them loading the yacht on the island."

"I don't think they really want you dead even though Brimm said he did, it never made sense. You're the answer to finding the treasure. I think they want to kidnap you to make you help them."

"Are you sure?"

"Think about it," he said. "They could've killed us in the ocean, but they didn't." He grimaced. "I've been so stupid, they were herding us back to Chicago, all along. I think they want you to find the artifact for them."

"But they shot at me?"

"And they missed, they just wanted to scare you. Johnson dove in front of you and caught that bullet, but I bet it would have hit the wall beside you."

The car lurched to a halt in emergency parking. "Let's go," he said, at the same time that they both jumped out and managed to follow Johnson inside on the gurney. He was still conscious and trying to joke with the EMTs but ended up coughing and gasping for breath.

Sloan grabbed Raven's hand and pulled her along with him, his full attention was on Johnson. Or at least that's what she thought until his hand squeezed hers reassuringly as they swept through the doors into the beehive of activity in the emergency room.

A nurse stopped them from following into the exam room. "Please, wait until the doctor sees him. In the meantime, can you give the desk clerk any pertinent information on the patient?"

"Sure, sure." A muscle worked in Sloan's jaw. It was evident he wanted to be where the action was, with his friend.

Raven waited in a chair while he told the nurse everything he could. He even knew his partner's insurance information.

It seemed like forever before he dropped into the chair beside her and looked at his watch. "Damnit, this is going to be a long night."

"Are you going to call Johnson's family? What's his first name by the way?"

"Johnson."

"Really? What's his last name, then?"

"Carver. And no, I'm not calling his family. Long story, I can't tell you right now."

"More secrets? You seem to be overburdened with them don't you?"

His expression didn't change. "We all have secrets, Raven. Even you."

"That's what's bothering me the most, especially since you think I might inadvertently know something that could help solve this thing." She shifted her position in the waiting room chair. "I really don't think I know anything, but I've decided to help you. I don't want those bastards to get whatever it is they're after." Not to mention, Johnson had taken that bullet to protect her and she owed him.

They watched two police officers go into the emergency room. They were only in Johnson's room for a few minutes before they left. Raven had been on edge, she expected them take her in for questioning but they didn't even ask about her.

"What's going on? Why didn't they want to see me?"

"Knowing Johnson, he didn't tell them you were there. He's very good at his job and he knows we need to solve this thing before the bad guys do. He put them off our scent."

She thought about Johnson's dedication. Would she be that dedicated under the same circumstances? Sheesh.

An hour later the nurse motioned them to her counter. "Your friend is going into surgery. He won't be out for a few hours and there's no real need for you to sit here. You should go home for now. Just leave your phone number and we'll contact you when he's out of surgery."

Sloan rubbed his head thoughtfully. "Is there any chance he might not make it?"

"The bullet didn't do as much damage as the doctor first feared. He's optimistic about the results of surgery."

"Thank you." He handed the nurse a card with his cell

phone number on it.

They returned to the vehicle and Raven buckled herself in. She'd been considering everything that had happened tonight, and while they were backing out of the parking space, she asked, "I'm a little confused. These people you work for, did they hire you to protect me?"

"I was specifically hired to find the location of the missing key or the artifact."

"But you had Johnson watching me?"

"I had to make sure you didn't turn up and blow my cover." He grinned. "But you did that anyway."

"And you tied me up and taped my mouth and threw me in a closet."

He flinched. "Pantry," he corrected. "Do you have to put it quite like that? I like to think I did that to save your skin. You wouldn't have believed that a stranger was trying to protect you especially after Captain Mike had a gun on you. I didn't have a choice, I had to get you out of harm's way quickly before you tipped one of them off to your presence."

"I guess I understand."

"Good, because the men your husband hooked up with are extremely dangerous. They have no conscience. All they care about is fattening their wallets."

"And the people you work for?" she asked, watching his hands grip the steering wheel.

"Powerful, yes, but very true to their beliefs."

The whole thing was just too bizarre. "So my parents really were members of this Protectorate?"

He nodded but kept his eyes on the road and the review mirror.

"Why would my parents want to be involved in something like that?"

"It's an honor to be a member family of this group. They've been protecting information and treasures for generations, since the earliest time of Knights Templar. They would have wanted you to be a member when you were old enough to decide. And for generations it's been easy, there's been no real danger because no one knew about us until Barry blabbed."

"Barry's greed got people murdered," she said with a frown. Barry wouldn't have been very old when her parents died. Only twenty-one. Had he been evil even then? "What do we do next?"

Sloan gripped the steering wheel tighter. "Tomorrow you will have to start racking your brains to try to figure out where the artifact might be. Even though Barry had followed a lead to the island, he learned something here in Chicago that led him there. Some bit of information we need to find. If we can find it we might have better luck."

"Damn that man! He took me away from my home, from Uncle Phil, and then he spent his time back here in Chicago?" She'd married a monster.

Sloan braked the car sharply and Raven slammed her palms onto the dash to stop her forward momentum. "Your uncle!" he said.

"Yes?"

"Where did he live?"

"On Gladiator Lane in the suburbs. It was such a shock when he fell off the roof he was re-shingling," she said with tears burning behind her eyes.

"Phil probably didn't know what hit him," Sloan said.

"You think Barry killed him don't you?" Her stomach balked at that thought.

"If Phil got in the way of his search, I'm afraid it's possible."

Her breath caught in her throat and she felt like a hole had been carved into her chest.

CHAPTER EIGHT

THEY REACHED Uncle Phil's house at midnight.

"Do you still own this?" Sloan asked pulling up in front of the old house.

She nodded. She hadn't had the heart to sell the house after her uncle's death. Not only did it hold memories of him, but her uncle had also kept her parents things in the attic.

"You lived here?" Sloan asked.

"Uncle Phil was my guardian. He did the best he could. He was an old bachelor trying to raise a heartbroken teenager. Unfortunately, I didn't make it easy for him."

She used to go into the attic and rummage through her parents' furniture and clothes. Just a whiff of their scent could bring their smiling faces back to her. She wasn't sure when she began to avoid her parents' things, but it had been a long time ago. "This old house is all that's left of my family," she said.

"I know what that feels like, Raven, I was raised by extended family members. They might have actually cared about me, but not in the same way my own parents would have."

She had the feeling he'd just shared something he didn't tell many people.

"Sorry to hear that, but my situation wasn't like that. Uncle Phil loved me as much as my own parents did," she said. "What happened to your parents?"

"My mother was murdered and my father was sent to prison for killing her. He was subsequently found hanged."

"Your father murdered your mother and hanged himself in prison?"

His expression darkened. "I don't believe he did it because he adored my mother. He would have done anything for her. And, I don't believe he hanged himself either because he'd never have left me to the relatives, he didn't even like most of them."

Raven swallowed. Her throat had gone completely dry. His story, intermingled with the feelings and memories this house elicited was enough to send her into a funk.

"Do you have a key to the house?" he asked while he parked the car in the back where it would be out of sight.

"I carry it with me, always. It's practically my good luck piece." She pulled the key chain out of her purse and eyed the pewter Celtic cross. "Considering what I've gone through the last few days, it looks like my good luck charm is working."

He nodded but seemed intent on assessing the house.

The trees around the property were overgrown and shabby and needed work desperately. Guilt at not being there for Uncle Phil mingled with melancholy at the familiar creak of the verandah steps as she approached the front door. Her throat tightened. The old oak door with its beautiful stained glass window looked dull now but in her youth the dragonflies and irises danced to life at night, sparkling with color and intensity from interior illumination. It had always felt magical to her as a child.

"Are you okay to go inside?" he asked.

"Of course I am," she lied. "If there's something here that will lead us to the truth, I'm need to find out. I'd like to move on with my life."

She waited while he unlocked the door. She stepped forward to enter but he blocked her with one arm.

"Normally, I'd say ladies first, but in this case I think you'd better let me go just in case."

Her heart fluttered. If anyone had damaged her uncle's belongings she'd be crushed. The old furniture had been so well taken care of, and what of the antique dishes that had belonged to her grandmother? Why hadn't she come back here sooner?

Inside, the house exuded an aura of dark depression. Of course the electricity had been turned off after Uncle Phil had died and while a thick layer of dust covered everything, it still smelled like home.

Sloan had a tiny flashlight he'd retrieved from the dash of his car. He pointed a thin beam of light around the room. "Seems safe. I think we're alone," he said.

"How would you know that already, you haven't even looked everywhere yet?"

He pointed the beam at the floor. "Floor's got a film of dust on it. He rubbed the toe of his shoe across the hardwood and Raven saw the mark in the dust. "No one's been across these floors for quite a while." He gave her a curious look, as if he wanted to know why she hadn't come home. At least he had the decency not to ask.

"What do you think we'll be able to accomplish here tonight?" she asked, wrapping her arms around herself and shivering. Maybe she wasn't ready for this after all.

"Probably nothing tonight. But we can start first thing in the morning. And, there's an added benefit, you won't be in your apartment if our friends come back."

"I didn't realize you'd want to stay here overnight," she said, moving further into the house. She didn't need the flashlight; she knew by heart where every piece of furniture sat. She ran a hand over the familiar Persian rug hanging on the wall on their way down the hallway toward the kitchen.

"Where are you going?" he asked.

"There should be a hurricane lamp under the sink in the kitchen. If we're staying the night we might as well have light. She reached into the cupboard and grabbed the antique cut-glass lantern, still full of oil. In a nearby drawer, she found matches and handed them to Sloan.

"Will you light it while I go light the fireplace?"

He suggested she take the flashlight, but she didn't need it. She'd spent many, many nights wandering around this house in the dark after her parents died. Hearing uncle Phil's snoring had become a constant in her life. She missed him terribly.

She went to the copper wood-box in the corner and took out some kindling and two logs that had been stacked neatly inside. She knew the box would be full because Uncle Phil always kept it that way. Even in the summer.

She opened the flue and had the kindling in place and a small fire started by the time Sloan came into the room with the Hurricane lamp lit.

He moved the lamp back and forth, surveying the room. "This place is a treasure trove of antiques."

"Are you thinking the artifact you're looking for could be here? In plain sight?"

He tipped his head in her direction. "You're very quick, Ms. Delacoeur, I'm sure you've been told that before."

She liked hearing her maiden name on his lips. "Only my uncle, but he thought the sun rose and set on me. This old house brings back so many memories," she said on a sigh.

"Is that why you haven't been back here until today?" He walked the perimeter of the room, shining the lamp on each surface and wall.

"How'd you know that?" she asked moving one of the wingback chairs next to the fireplace. It was summer, but the house felt cold inside. "Because of the dust on the floors?"

"That, and I could tell by your reaction when we entered the house. You haven't been home since your uncle died, have you?" He stopped near the fireplace and illuminated a picture of Raven and her Uncle on the mantle.

* * * * *

Sloan wanted to let the light linger on Raven's image, but at the intake of her breath he moved to another location. This was going to be a trying night for her.

"How did you have the strength to go to Heart's Devotion?"

A strangled sound caught in her throat. "What did you just say? Heart's Devotion?"

"The house on the island, that's what it's called. Didn't you see the name on the plaque over the door?"

"No, I didn't notice it. But then I entered at gunpoint and exited through the upstairs window, so that might be why I missed it." She frowned. "There's something familiar about that name, but I can't put my finger on it." She grabbed a poker and moved one of the partially burning logs.

"So you decided to risk coming to the island, because?" He'd given up on finding anything in the living room, so he seated himself on an old wooden rocker.

"I've already told you it was because I wanted to know if Barry was still alive."

The rocking chair creaked under Sloan. "And now that you know, do you feel better?"

She dusted off the sofa before she sat. "I wish I'd stayed at home and remained oblivious."

"Are you sure that's true?" She lived for adventure, whether she knew it or not. "You realize if we're successful in finding the artifact, we can get those idiots off your back."

"Let me get this straight," she said. "You think Barry came back here every time he told me he was on a business trip? If that's true, why didn't Uncle Phil tell me?"

"I'm guessing by that time Phil knew how dangerous Barry was. I'd guess he didn't tell you because he wanted to keep you safe. Maybe he died because he was going to tell you about Barry. From what you say about your uncle, his world revolved around you, he'd protect you at all costs."

Even from here he could see tears glistening in her eyes. Smooth, Brockway!

"If that's true, then it was my fault uncle Phil died." A moan escaped her and she sagged in her chair.

"Your uncle was as much a target as you were, Raven. He housed your parents' things. He protected secrets. He knew what he was up against because he was one of us."

She sniffed. "Then why did my family leave me out of the information loop?"

"After your parents died you were young and traumatized. I imagine your uncle wanted to wait until he felt you were ready to hear the truth."

Her angry expression surprised him. "He should've told me before I got married."

"Unless he'd decided the family secret was too dangerous and had cost too much already. Maybe he didn't want that for you. Your mother was his sister, wasn't she? His baby sister? Maybe he didn't want to risk losing you, too."

Her head jerked up and she squinted at Sloan. "What is this secret? Don't you think it's time you told me?" She jumped to her feet, her hands fisted. "In fact, I demand that you tell me right now." Her voice wobbled and her blue eyes were almost luminescent in the lamplight.

Pushing out of the chair felt like it took all his energy. He needed to put some distance between himself and Raven because he wanted to pull her into his arms and make everything better. Since he couldn't do that for her, he paced to the window and stared outside. While Phil's house sat in this neighborhood unused and uncared for, the rest of the neighbors went on with their lives without giving a thought to the ghosts in this house.

He thought of his own family giving everything for The Protectorate. He'd been raised to believe they'd been recruited to save the world's most precious antiquities for the betterment of mankind. Sloan's cousin Victor had tarnished his family name within The Protectorate when he killed Raven's parents in an attempt to get to the treasure they protected. Now, Sloan wanted to repair the family name, at least for his parents' sake.

Suddenly he realized Raven had been abnormally quiet. Damnation—she'd nearly been killed by an assassin only hours before and he'd brought her back to the one place she felt safe until he told her that her uncle had probably been murdered by her husband. What the hell was wrong with him! Right now he'd prefer to see her smile, but he'd made sure that wouldn't happen. Dumb ass.

While he tried to come up with a way to make it up to her, she got up and stood next to him at the window. "What do you see out there?" she asked in a whisper.

"Shadows of the past," he said, gritting his teeth against his stupidity.

"Oh," she said. He heard every bit of the pain she felt at his thoughtless words.

He'd reminded her of her heartbreak all over again.

"I'm sorry Raven," he said, touching her shoulders and turning her to face him. He knew he shouldn't, but he couldn't stop himself—he tipped her chin up and kissed her in an exploratory, tentative kiss.

At first she didn't yield to him, in fact she froze. For a second he thought he'd made a mistake until her mouth opened to him, and the kiss deepened. She pressed herself against him, and wrapped her arms around his neck and held on tight.

The kiss lasted until they were both breathless. He shouldn't have kissed her—she didn't know everything about him—she didn't remember. He couldn't lose her now. Still his mouth moved of its own volition against her soft, deliciously scented skin, down her neckline across her collarbone.

She turned the tables against him by kissing him into submission, testing his strength of will to its limit. He reveled in the taste of her, the ecstasy of her. He barely managed to gather the ability to gently pull away before it was too late, before she hated him for this moment when she learned the truth.

Before he could divulge everything they had to find the artifact to make her monsters go away. Now that she was aware of him, he'd do whatever he could to protect her, even though he couldn't tell her who he really was. He couldn't let his feelings for her affect how he handled this job. Her safety depended on it.

It seemed that the kiss had taken Raven's mind off her family for a moment, but it had taken a piece of his soul in the interim.

CHAPTER NINE

RAVEN WOKE in the middle of the night. The air felt stuffy and hot in the downstairs bedroom, she shouldn't have built a fire in the fireplace in the middle of summer. Despite the heat, she pulled the sheets up to her neck. Had she heard breathing? The stale air suddenly seemed overpowering and probably caused the headache germinating at the back of her eyes. She stifled a moan.

What had woken her? Wait—it had been a familiar sound—the way Barry always tapped his index finger on his belt buckle. Tap, tap, tap—but it couldn't have been him, he was dead. She knew that now. Still, she felt fuzzy and kind of strange, it must have been a dream.

Her breath froze in her throat when the darkness changed, mutated into a hazy purple shape growing closer until a familiar outline loomed over her. Had the tapping she'd heard been the pounding of her heart? Or was it Barry in the room with her?

She squeezed her eyelids closed. "No! You're dead. It can't be you." She started to cry, until heartrending howls spilled out of her and the shadow dissipated and blew away like a soft mist in a light breeze. Gone, but the danger remained palpable, it hadn't gone away.

Someone shook her.

"Raven. Wake up."

She jerked upright and the sheet fell away. "No. You're dead," she said, remnants of her dream clinging to her like stale perfume.

"It's me, Sloan." He pulled her toward him, and wrapped his arms around her even while she tried to struggle out of his grasp. Finally realizing it wasn't Barry, she pressed her face into his chest and sobbed. "I thought I heard him. I could smell him, and even worse, I felt his presence. He was here. In this room with me."

"Who was here?" Sloan sounded upset.

"Barry."

Sloan released an angry breath. "It was just a dream, Raven. Even if someone got in, he couldn't have escaped without me seeing him. I heard you calling out in your sleep and came right away."

"Are you sure?" She pushed away from him and looked at his outline aided by the dim light filtering into her room from the street. The concern etching his features was more real than the shadow of her dreams. "Are you sure he wasn't here?"

"Positive."

He held her in his arms until she stopped trembling.

"I'm okay, you can let go of me," she said, still raw from the dream. "I haven't had that bad dream for a couple of months—being here must've brought it on again. I'm not sure why this house would cause my nightmare to reoccur, I was happy here with uncle Phil."

Sloan walked to the window and pulled back the curtains until the streetlight illuminated the side of his face. "I'm not him, you know."

"Pardon?" With her back against the headboard now and her knees up against her chest, she yanked the blankets up to her chin to ward off the growing chill that threatened to ravage her. She knew exactly what he was saying.

"I'm not Barry," he said again.

"I know you're not Barry, but your life revolves around the same thing, doesn't it? You hunt for treasure, you take risks and you live for the danger—you might as well be him."

Sloan winced. She'd struck a blow with that last statement, and it obviously cut deep.

"I would never do anything to hurt you, Raven, that

means I'm not like him at all."

"I'm sorry but I only have your word for that. You can't deny you've got the same fever in your blood, I've seen it before and you don't even need to explain it to me now because my parents were just like you, weren't they? Treasure hunters." She believed that now.

"They were protectors, Raven. It's not the same."

"But their lives revolved around treasure, didn't it? They'd become consumed with it. If they'd lived a normal life, they'd still be alive."

He let the curtain drop. "Nothing is guaranteed in this life, Raven. They could've been killed some other way. No one can predict if they'd still be alive. But they believed in what they did, so much so, they wanted it for you, too."

She sighed. "Maybe I put too much of the blame on them, I don't know. I've tried to get a clearer picture of them in my memories."

He moved back to the bed and adjusted her sheet. "Try to go back to sleep, I'll stay here with you, if that'll help."

"No way," she said.

"I'll sleep on the lounge in front of the window, then. Far enough away? If you're not alone, you'll probably sleep better. Now try to relax and close your eyes and do what you're told for once." There was humor in his comment; otherwise, she would have kicked him out.

She must've fallen asleep again because when she woke the next time to see a shadow rising off the lounge, she whispered. "Sloan?"

"Quiet, don't make a sound. Someone is upstairs."

Her initial reaction was to jump up and get dressed. He motioned her back down and pressed a finger over his lips. "Shh."

A floorboard creaked somewhere on the second floor. She carefully moved onto her knees and now she wondered if it had been a dream earlier, or reality.

Another floorboard creaked above, hopefully caused by the unheated building shifting?

Sloan stood near the doorway, listening. He didn't look like someone who thought the noises were mere boards creaking.

"Stay put," he mouthed before slipping into the hall at the base of the stairs, and disappearing up the steps.

Seconds later she heard a thump upstairs. Sloan?

How had Sloan had managed to get upstairs without making a sound? How was it that he knew which steps would be silent and which one would creak and give him away? Had he been in her uncle's house before, too?

She hated this feeling of distrust. Her mind kept telling her to trust no one, but she wanted to trust Sloan. She cursed her lack of judgment, hadn't she learned anything from Barry?

Creeping up the stairs might not be the best time to think about Uncle Phil's last day alive, but she couldn't stop herself. Had he woken in his sleep and heard similar noises? His bedroom had been upstairs—had they broken his neck and thrown him off the roof to make it look like an accident? Had he been murdered?

Scraping noises continued above. Obviously, whoever was in the house had no idea they weren't alone. Halfway up the stairs she heard a curse then a slam, then the sound of scuffling.

With her heart beating like crazy, she managed to reach the landing without giving herself away. She spotted someone in the hallway not far from where she stood. She couldn't quite make out his shape in the dim light from the bedroom windows. "Sloan?"

"Raven, get back downstairs." Sloan's voice echoed through the upper rooms but not from the direction of the person she was looking at.

Her muscles tightened. "I'm calling the police," she

shouted in a stupid attempt to scare the stranger off.

It was like poking an angry bear. Charging her and cursing virulently, he shoved her hard enough that her feet slid along the hardwood floor toward the open stairwell. She couldn't stop her backward momentum no matter how hard she clawed for a place to hang on. He intended to shove her to her death.

Desperate to save herself, she grabbed him by the arms and prepared to throw him. It was the only move she'd semi-mastered before she'd quit her Marshal Arts class. If she could knock the air out of him, she'd chop across his throat next, or knee him in the groin. Unfortunately, her lack of experience failed when he countered her move, forcing her toward the top of the stairs again. Panicking and not daring to look around to see how close she was to a fatal fall, she screamed, "Sloan, help."

"He can't help you, bitch."

Chills spiked up her spine and she tried to see where the stairs were. Too close—she grabbed for the railing before he gave her the final shove that would send her to her death.

Failing, her attacker reeled out another string of vile curses then tried to pry her off the spindles.

Her arms felt like they were being pulled out of their sockets but she hung on. Where was Sloan? "Sloan, Sloan. Help me!"

No response. "Let me go you bastard!"

He laughed. Another yank and she cried out in pain even though she didn't want to give him the satisfaction.

"You're gonna' take the same header off the roof that your dear departed uncle took, bitch," he said. "Should've been you in the first place since you ain't been nothin' but trouble."

If she'd carried out her parents' wishes and had studied self-defense, she'd be able to save herself right now. In a spurt of panic she wrapped her legs round her attacker's legs and flipped herself sideways.

It worked. He lost his balance and toppled down the steps.

Her overworked muscles felt like clay when she clamored to get to the top of the stairs again. She'd just made it when her attacker came thundering back up.

With him on her heels, she tore down the hall and had almost made it to Uncle Phil's room to lock the door between them, when both of his hands wrapped around her neck and he started squeezing from behind.

It was the end—she couldn't breathe. Where was Sloan?

Her limbs sagged and she started seeing fireworks behind her eyes.

Suddenly, the pressure released and her attacker flipped past her and landed on the hardwood floor on his back. She dropped onto her knees on the floor gasping for breath.

Sloan's shape hovered over her and he touched her shoulder. "You okay, doll?"

She nodded but her throat burned and she couldn't speak.

It looked like her attacker was out cold. When she looked at Sloan he had a piece of wood in his hands. He'd broken a carving over the guy's head.

Suddenly another man lurched out of the shadows. "Watch out," she managed to rasp out.

Sloan reacted instantly and countered the attack. It was easy to tell he hadn't quit his training. His movements were smooth and quick when he slashed the attacker and dropped the man to his knees.

"You've got some explaining to do, asshole," Sloan said between labored breaths.

Raven had barely managed to get to her feet when a third person burst out of Uncle Phil's bedroom and dropped a canister on the floor.

Sloan let go of the guy he'd been pommeling and dove for her instantly. He grabbed her and rolled with her toward Uncle Phil's bedroom covering her body with his own. The explosion felt like it pierced her eardrums while light filled the house even though her eyes were closed.

The weight of his body holding her down felt permanent. He didn't move. Was he dead?

"Sloan. Sloan." She tried to push him off her. "Are you okay?"

She couldn't feel his breathing when she tried to get out from under him. Maybe she was panicking because when she screamed his name, he rolled off of her.

"Raven, I'm sorry, did I hurt you?" He helped her sit up.

"How can you be alive? The grenade!"

"It was only a flash-bang, a device used to debilitate. Those idiots were more prepared than I gave them credit for. I'm afraid they got away." He looked around. "They even managed to drag the unconscious guy out, damn it."

Sloan rubbed at the back of his head and she realized he hadn't come when she'd called for him because they'd knocked him out. Good thing he had a hard head.

"I thought I was all alone again," she rasped through her strained vocal chords. "I thought you were dead."

He pulled her close. "Good thing I'm tougher than I look," he said with a hint of humor in his voice. He smiled at her just long enough to make her want to smile back, but instead she shoved him away and got to her feet.

"Let's go get the lantern. Maybe we can find out what those men were looking for. I want this over with and the sooner the better," she said.

His gaze said it all. He understood how she felt.

Back in the living room she got a better look at him, blood dripped freely from his split eyebrow. He blinked and rubbed blood out of his eye.

"You're more hurt than I realized," she said.

"I hate to admit that the first guy distracted me while the second one got the drop. I was knocked out for a bit." He touched his head. "I must've gone head first into something."

"No wonder you didn't hear me call for you," she said.

His frown turned darker. "It's not very often someone gets the better of me and I'm not in the least bit amused."

"Do you think they're really gone?"

"I'm pretty sure they're gone," he said swiping the blood away from his eye. "And I don't think they'll be back tonight."

"I bet they didn't expect anyone else to be here," she said, holding the light up to see his forehead better. "You might need stitches."

"I think I'll live."

"It's bleeding quite a bit," she said, biting her lip.

"This type of cut always bleeds. It's no big deal."

His shoulders tightened when she continued to survey his wound and until his intake of breath she'd been oblivious to the chemistry sizzling between them. She started to back away gracefully until he leaned toward her and kissed her.

The unexpected kiss after a near death experience— pure ecstasy. Okay, if she was honest with herself she felt the chemistry between them no matter how hard she'd tried to ignore it. It was total insanity, especially since Sloan had admitted to wanting the same thing as her husband. What made him any different?

* * * * *

Sloan slowly edged her back onto the couch. He'd regret this later. Even though he risked everything by doing this and scaring her away, he didn't stop himself. He needed this as much as she needed answers.

Any soldier knew near death experience could cause a person to do things they wouldn't do normally. And, the second kiss tonight was probably a direct result of escaping death again. Regardless, her kisses were pure heaven, her lips soft and so sweet, and the tiny little moan she'd just made nearly sent him over the edge.

If he took advantage of her now, he'd never be able to forgive himself. She still didn't know the shameful secret his family held, a secret irreparably linked to her past.

Against his better judgment, he ran a hand down her curves, slid his thumb along the edge of her breast where his hand lingered until he forced himself to step away.

Too bad they'd both been born into families whose lives were indentured into service to a cause many of their ancestors had lived and died for. No one ever got out, or wanted out because it was as old and privileged an honor as one could imagine, and a heavy burden to carry in the modern world. No one had double-crossed The Protectorate for generations until Barry and his brother. They'd changed everything.

"Raven, I'm sorry. I shouldn't have…" He inched away from her, then got up and strode to the bay window. "Let's promise each other to forget what just happened, okay?" he said in a monotone. "You don't trust me and you have good reason."

She stared at him, confusion evident in her features.

It was then, in the muted light of the oil lantern, he could see dark bruising on her neck. "Raven! You're the one who's hurt, why didn't you tell me?"

Her fingers flicked to her neck. "I'll live," she said in a rough voice, echoing his mantra.

Why hadn't he noticed the rasp in her voice? He couldn't forgive the fact that he'd let his desire do all the thinking. What a bastard he was. He slammed one fist against the windowsill and dust billowed up.

His gut clenched. Was he any better than Barry? He was using her too. He needed her to find the artifact, but at what cost? Not to use Raven the way Barry had.

But wasn't that exactly what he was doing?

CHAPTER TEN

RAVEN WATCHED Sloan from her position on the sofa. What was he thinking right now? That he'd made a mistake by kissing her? Imagine scaredy-cat Raven Delacoeur tempting a big, tough guy like him. But, oh, she knew she'd tempted him, there was no denying his reaction to her. Whatever his reasons, he wanted her. And as crazy as it was, the feeling was mutual.

"You saved my life tonight," she began and he winced visibly. No doubt he thought she'd kissed him because she felt grateful. Maybe in some part that was true.

"I nearly cost you your life," he said bitterly.

"You threw yourself on top of me to protect me from a grenade." Something played across his face at the mention of the grenade.

"Not a grenade, a flash-bang. I saved you from temporary blindness and that's about all. It's the fact that those goons got the drop on me that really ticks me off, I know better than to get myself ambushed. And, because of my carelessness, you were nearly choked to death. You should see the bruises on your throat."

His voice got husky, he sounded like that when he couldn't cover up his anger or his emotions. She was beginning to understand him.

"I'll find something to put on your eyebrow," she said. "Maybe some antibacterial salve for your bullet wound, too?" She needed a distraction right now and turning the focus back onto him worked for her, and it didn't hurt to remind him how heroic he'd been.

He touched his brow with two fingers and brought them back red with blood. His cut wasn't bleeding profusely any more, but it was still bleeding.

"Just a piece of some kind of tape will probably work if your uncle has anything in the house." He paused. "What about you? Do you want to go to the hospital and have your windpipe checked?"

"No thanks. It'd be hard to explain and I don't want to end up talking to the police all night. I have the feeling you don't want me to, either." She swallowed and felt her throat muscles contract painfully. "It'll just take time for the bruising to go away."

Sloan knew she was right. When the cops saw the bruises on her throat, it would raise questions they didn't want to answer. It would be too risky at this point.

"Let's just take a look and see if we can find something to cover that cut," she said. "Uncle Phil was always prepared for anything. There must be a first aid box in this house." She should know where to find it. "Wait, I know where it is, it's in the first floor bathroom under the sink."

She found a small butterfly bandage and some salve and handed it to him, careful not to touch him this time.

He looked disappointed—too bad. She watched while he used the small mirror and lamplight to press the bandage over his cut. Then she handed him a towel so he could wipe away the excess blood before it dried. He slapped the towel roughly across his face and she winced.

Before she could say a thing, he'd turned and stalked out of the tiny room. Since he had the only light, she followed him.

"Do you think they found what they were looking for?" she asked.

"Doubt it. We interrupted their fun."

Her heart skipped a beat. "Then whatever it is could still be here?"

"It could." He didn't sound excited by that fact. "Problem is we have no idea what it is or where it might be hidden. We might find it and disregard it."

"Maybe something will look familiar to you?" she said. Sloan had obviously done research on her family, on the so-called Protectorate. She doubted she'd be able to help but was willing to try. "One thing I know, I'm not going to sleep again any time soon. At least keeping busy will calm my jangled nerves."

"Are you sure you feel up to searching the house tonight? You've taken quite a bashing."

She did have a few sore spots that would probably be worse by tomorrow, but for now, she needed to keep herself busy. "You're the one who got cracked on the back of the head and cut on the eyebrow."

He grunted. "Point made. We're good to go." He stopped at the bottom of the stairs and extended a hand for her to go first. "I'll be right behind you."

"I wish we both had a light so we could look in different locations," she said at the top of the stairs. His little penlight wouldn't help much. "Wait, Uncle Phil always had extra flashlights around the house in case the power went out. I think there's a light in my old bedroom upstairs." She shouldn't have mentioned her bedroom. She didn't know if she could face going in there again, the very same reason she'd used the spare bedroom downstairs tonight.

She halted at the bedroom door with Sloan close behind her.

"Shall we go in?"

"No. I don't think so," she said. "Too many memories—most of them best forgotten."

He stepped up to her. "Want me to go in?"

She bit her lip. She hated being such an idiot. "Would you mind?"

It surprised her that he was sensitive enough to realize how she felt about this house, about her old bedroom.

"It's in my bed stand. There's a drawer with a silver flashlight inside."

He was back in seconds with the flashlight.

"Does it still work?"

He flicked the light on and handed it to her. "Where do you want to start?"

"What about Uncle Phil's room? It seems to be the place the criminals were most interested in."

He nodded and they made for the bedroom at the end of the hall.

"This is where they hit me with the board," he said, rubbing the back of his head as a reminder.

Uncle Phil's bedroom was a mess. Drawers pulled open, clothes tossed about. The familiar scents of her uncle's clothing caught in her throat. She really missed that gruff old guy who'd raised her to womanhood. It couldn't have been easy for him.

His mattress hung off the side of the bed frame, sliced open. "As if Uncle Phil would be dumb enough to hide something valuable in a mattress." She gritted her teeth. But where would he hide valuables? He was a crafty old guy. He even had a secret room in case someone broke into the house. That thought made her smile. She'd loved spending time in that room thinking no one could ever find her, other than Uncle Phil.

The secret room! Why hadn't she thought of that?

Sloan had been going through Phil's things when she reached out and grabbed his arm. His hair had been messed up by his scuffle earlier and the bandage over his right eye crinkled when his brows rose. "Find something?"

"No, but I've just remembered something important. I should have thought of it sooner."

"Okay?" His voice was smooth, questioning. He didn't push.

She took a long breath. "Can I really trust you?"

"Honey, you can trust me with your life. I'd never do

anything to deliberately hurt you. I wish I could prove that to you."

She sighed and realized he'd proven it to her on more than one occasion. "Okay. Here goes. Uncle Phil had a secret room!" she said.

Sloan's expression lightened. "Seriously? There was nothing in the blueprints for the house," he said almost to himself.

"Of course it wouldn't be in the blueprints. It wouldn't be secret then, would it?"

He chuckled at that. "You make a good point."

"It's out here in the hallway," Raven said, wondering if her life would ever be normal again.

She walked along the hall. Uncle Phil's house had been too big for a bachelor but he had meetings and guests all the time. His life had been very full and he enjoyed every minute of it. Knowing what she knew now, she guessed it was Protectorate meetings being held here.

She ran her hand along the dark wood paneling. Counting the lines as she went. When she found number twenty-three, she pushed in on the board and a latch clicked. A small panel opened and a biometric identification tool slid out of the box.

"Oh no. I've never seen this before. It must've been something Uncle Phil put in after I got married."

"I wonder why he did that?" Sloan said with a hint of derision in his voice.

Raven was stunned at the realization that her uncle had probably done it to keep Barry out. "Why didn't he just tell me he didn't trust Barry?"

"You were newly married. This was probably his safest bet, because even if you did happen to tell Barry about the secret room, and Barry was lucky enough to find it, he still wouldn't be able to get inside." Sloan grinned. "I wish I'd met your uncle. He and I would have got along, I think."

"That won't help us now. We can't get inside, either," she reminded.

"Your uncle wouldn't have done this unless there was a way for you to get inside, too. Your safety was his number one concern."

"I wonder how it works?"

"Finger print. See that mark in the center? Just the right size for a finger." He tapped his chin then reached out and gently took her index finger and pressed it on the glass screen.

They heard a click then the door opened.

"Very smart uncle indeed," he said. They stepped inside.

"It looks different than before." She stared at the metal on the walls and ceiling. "It used to be wood paneling not metal."

"I'd say no way was anyone getting in here unless they had your fingerprint, or his. And I'm pretty sure these walls mean it's secure in case of fire." He suddenly looked speculative.

"The artifact must be in here," she said.

He nodded but he still looked tense, the chords on his neck rigid. "Here's hoping. Let's look and see what we can find."

Raven had been inside this room many times after her parents' death. Back then she only had to push the right wooden panel and the door opened. Her uncle had told her not to keep coming here, but she had anyway. There was something about the place that drew her back again and again. He'd found her here a few times and never got angry. Smelling like peppermints, he'd pat her on the head and tell her the room shouldn't be used except for emergencies. As if his watery blue eyes were smiling down on her right now, welcoming her, she scanned the room again. As a teenager these so-called treasures looked like nothing but junk to her, nothing but old papers and ancient keepsakes that no one would ever want. But now... Now, these papers and antiques were something even she could tell were valuable.

"This could take a while," she said. The room was stacked with antiques of every kind.

Sloan looked grim at the indomitable task ahead. "We could be here for a week."

Raven wandered around the room, touching a vase and fondling an old coin lying on top of a desk in the corner. She looked through the drawers and found a manifest of the items in the room. She glanced at it but saw nothing that struck her as a key to an artifact. She started to hand it to Sloan when the words "diary" caught her eye at the bottom of the page. "Mom's diary is in this room somewhere. It's not what we're looking for but I'd love to have it."

"Unless we accidentally find the diary, I think you'd better focus on our task at hand, we don't have a lot of time, especially now that Brimm's men know we're here. We've got to find the artifact as soon as possible if we hope to have any chance at solving this thing."

"Understood," she said, and she did understand, but her spirits flagged because to her the diary was the treasure, it contained her mother's words and thoughts. Maybe it held a clue to why her parents worked for The Protectorate. Maybe it held a message for her.

* * * * *

Sloan moved the lantern to the middle of the room so they could both see a little better. He'd heard the disappointment in her voice and it caught him in the chest. He knew what that diary probably meant to her, but in order to save her they needed the artifact more at this point. They'd come back and find the diary later.

"Yeah, that's the hard part. I don't have any idea what the artifact might be. I just hope we'll know it when we see it, but I'm afraid that's probably not going to be likely. Just tell me if you see anything that looks like a map, or a key, or anything that seems out of place."

When she suddenly laughed, he jerked his head up from the cupboard he was digging in. Had she cracked from all of the stress? "Raven?"

"Everything in here seems out of place to me. Who'd want this stuff?"

Sloan scanned the room with reverence in his gaze. "This place is brimming with priceless wonders," he said. "I wish we had more time so I could tell you about some of the better pieces."

She laughed and held up an old bronze of some sort of ugly troll. "This for instance?"

His eyes twinkled and even he had to grin. "Well maybe some things were put here purely for your uncle's pleasure. Or for yours?"

She put the troll down and opened the bottom drawer of the desk and started going through every tedious little piece of paper and old bills. It seemed as if her uncle kept everything.

In the last drawer on the bottom right hand side, she'd just removed the files when she noticed something twinkling at the back of the drawer. She bent down. "I found something odd here," she said. "If there's no electricity in this house why is there a light flashing inside this drawer?"

Sloan sped to her side and dropped to the floor on his knees. He bent his head and examined the bottom drawer. "I'll be damned," he said. "You're uncle has a backup electrical system in this room."

He got up, searched the room and flicked on the light switch that they hadn't even bothered to try previously. Lights flared and the brightness in the room made them both blink.

He went back to the drawer. "This is a biometric switch, too. Try it."

"What if it's a booby trap and we blow ourselves up or something?"

Sloan sank back on his heels and smiled at her. "I really think you're cut out for this stuff," he said with humor in his voice. "I'm pretty sure it's okay and you're safe to give it a try."

She got down on her knees beside him. Shoulder against shoulder, they tried to get a good look inside the bottom drawer.

He couldn't even guess at how he'd feel in her position. It must be hard to wrap her brain around everything she'd learned about her family.

"Go ahead. Put your finger on the glass. This room has been created and safeguarded for the two of you. You're the only one capable of opening the door, short of tearing it apart; and I suspect if we tried that, whatever is inside would be destroyed before we could get to it."

She pressed her finger against the glass inside the drawer. They heard another pop, and a compartment between the two drawers in front slid open.

Sloan took out a leather box. Nestled inside on a piece of black velvet lay Raven's mother's diary.

CHAPTER ELEVEN

RAVEN KNEW what it was the minute she laid eyes on it. Her mother's initials were embossed on the leather cover in gold. The diary was beautiful and probably a gift from her father since Raven had received a smaller version when she'd turned thirteen. Her fingers traced the engraving.

"It's funny there are only a few pieces of paper in here besides mom's diary. Maybe the diary is the prized possession inside this box," Sloan said.

Her fingers caressed the leather. It gleamed with a patina of use and love. This had been her mother's, the last thing her mother would ever be able to tell her about herself.

"There is nothing more precious in this room, at least, not to me," she said.

Sloan reached into the back of the secret drawer and pulled out some long sheets stapled together in the corner with a blue triangle. He looked it over and grinned. "It's the deed to Heart's Devotion and the island itself—proof it belongs to you."

She watched the corners of his eyes crinkle when he smiled. She liked that about him, it meant he probably smiled often even though she hadn't seen much evidence of it since they'd met.

He had a kind face and somehow in the last forty-eight hours she'd made a decision to trust him.

Was gullibility still her middle name?

After Barry, she should never trust a single soul completely again.

Forgetting the diary for a moment, she took the Deed from him. Her parents' names were on the sheet in bold script. The island and the house had been in the family for two hundred years! She must have been there before. Why didn't she remember it?

She closed her eyes. Nothing. She remembered nothing. There were things about her past she'd forgotten, but that was normal, everyone forgets things. But this piece of paper was proof there was a gaping hole of information missing from her memory. This deed and the house on the island proved it.

"Tired?" Sloan asked.

She set the Deed down on the desk along with the diary and looked at the mountains of possible artifacts in front of them. "Not yet. You?"

He shook his head.

"Let's keep looking then."

Two hours later and covered in dust, and with the diary clutched safely in her hands, they left the room and reset the lock.

"I'm exhausted," she said touching her sore throat. It was getting quite tender and she was very thirsty.

Sloan lifted the lantern higher to get a look at her and swore through his teeth. "Damn it, Raven. That's looks nasty. Maybe we should take you to the hospital, after all. Does it hurt?"

She swallowed. "Not too bad. I just think my skin is bruised." She descended the stairs, aiming for the kitchen. "I am thirsty though. I'm going to get a drink of water." They'd picked up bottled water on their way here and had left it in the kitchen.

Sloan pushed the button on his watch and it cast an eerie luminescent glow in the upstairs hallway. "It's two o'clock in the morning. After you get your drink, we'd better try to get some sleep. Maybe we'll find something else in the hidden room after we've had a chance to rest and can look with fresh eyes."

She heaved a tired breath then yawned. "Maybe we should go somewhere else for the rest of the night?"

"I'm pretty sure those idiots won't be back here tonight, but just in case, I'm not leaving this place vacant for them to do their searching."

"Uncle Phil has a few guns in the house," she said.

"Does he?"

"There's a cabinet in the back room." She rubbed her nose. Digging around in the dust in the secret room made her face a little itchy.

"Is the cabinet locked?"

"Yes, but I remember where he kept the key."

One eyebrow arched. "He told a teenager where the key to the weapons was kept?"

"No. I imagined myself a junior sleuth back then. I thought it was my job to solve every mystery. It took me weeks to find the key, but I did eventually."

"Lead on Holmes," he said with a grin.

She went to the umbrella holder near the front door. Along with the umbrellas were several canes. She lifted out a cane with a brass bulldog head. Popping the head off, she knocked the key out of the hole inside, it fell into her hand.

"Must've taken you quite a while to find that!"

"I used to like to solve mysteries."

He nodded as if he understood. "I hope you still do, because we've got a heck of a mystery to uncover yet."

She led him to the gun cabinet and unlocked it.

He whistled when he saw the rows and rows of pistols and rifles. "Now this is what I'd call well stocked." He reached in and extracted a Ruger P89. She knew the type because each gun was catalogued with name placards below.

She watched while he searched the upper cabinet until he found the clip that held the appropriate bullets. He loaded the gun, checked the weapon.

"Safety's on," he said. "If for some reason you need to

use the gun the safety is located here and here, it's on either side."

She noted the information, but promised herself never to touch the weapon.

Seeing the guns made her think of Johnson. "I wonder if Johnson is out of surgery? If he'll be okay?"

Sloan rubbed a weary hand over his face and slid the gun into his belt then relocked the cabinet and handed Raven the key. "The nurse said they'd call. But you're right, we should have heard by now." He pulled out his phone. "Maybe they left a voice mail message. I turned the ringer off when I heard noises upstairs." He flipped open the phone and listened to a couple of messages.

She knew the second he heard good news, his features smoothed out and he nodded his head.

"He made it through. They say he's already out of intensive care."

"Thank heavens," she said.

"I'll call him in the morning," Sloan said. "Right now we really should try to get some rest. We've got a long day ahead of us tomorrow."

Her steps faltered just before the first floor bedroom that she'd been sleeping in earlier. Sleep was the last thing on her mind right now because she wanted to read the diary, but she wouldn't tell Sloan. "Goodnight then."

"Night, Raven. Sleep tight." He turned and walked toward the living room.

She could hardly wait for him to leave. She had the lantern. This was her chance to feel a connection with her mother again.

Now, in bed, propped up against the pillows, she ran her fingers over the soft brown leather and stared at the golden clasp. A memory came back to her, a memory of her mother curled up on the couch writing in this book while Raven watched television.

Since Raven had a smaller version of this diary she knew the key was tucked into the binding in a little pocket. She found the tiny key and opened the clasp.

Her fingers were shaking when she opened the diary to the first page, to the long sloping script—so beautiful—so familiar. At first, she could hear Sloan moving around in the living room down the hall but before long she'd been captured by her mother's description of their daily lives. About Raven and how much she adored her little girl. Sniffing back tears, Raven continued reading. Occasionally her mother wrote about the adventures the three of them had. About spending summers on the island! She had been there! Why didn't she remember?

Her mother wrote about how much Raven loved the beach in the fog. How they always joked about the old homestead being their castle and Raven was the princess.

She dropped the diary onto her lap and stared at the wall in front of her without really seeing it. How was this possible? How could she forget a major portion of her existence?

Finally, she picked it up again and read on, a funny feeling in the pit of her stomach. It felt as if this journal described someone else's life. She had no memory of the island, not even a tiny shred of it.

Before she went any further, she closed the diary and padded down the hall to Sloan. Maybe he could suggest a reason for the discrepancies in her mother's journal. How could she have ever been on that island as a child and not remember it? If she hadn't recognized her mother's handwriting she might have believed it was a fake, but that writing was so familiar and the tone of the writing was definitely her mother's.

Sloan had stretched out on the couch. His hands were propped behind his head and he was staring at the ceiling until he turned his head to look at her. "Anything wrong?"

She shook her head. "No. And I have a very good

reason to come here," she said. "I've been reading my mother's journal and there are things in here that don't make sense." Diary in hand, she held it out to him.

He sat up and took it from her but didn't open it.

"Sit beside me," he said patting the cushion. His hair was ruffled as if he'd been running his fingers through it. It made him look almost boyish—tousled and handsome but still dangerous. She couldn't forget that part.

"What did you find that doesn't make sense?"

"That stupid island. My mother actually talks about it in her journal. She said I loved it there." She clapped her hands on her face and propped her elbows on her knees and stared at her feet. "The thing is, I don't remember ever being there before a few days ago. Why would my mother say that?"

His expression shifted to something that looked very much like pity. She gritted her teeth.

"You don't have any recollection of the place?" he asked, his voice cautious, questioning, as if he thought she should remember it too.

"I have no recollection of ever being there." She hesitated. "Except for one moment of déjà vu when Mike pushed me inside that house. For just a second I thought the place looked familiar but I realized that foyers are similar in tons of old houses. I could've seen one somewhere else."

His expression softened. "Or maybe you remember that house. Just a little."

"Why would I forget an island and a house that by all account I'd spent summers visiting?" Raven slumped back against the cushions. In fact, she didn't remember many summer vacations at all. "I think I'm losing my mind, Sloan." She pressed two fingers against the bridge of her nose to stop the stinging sensation at the back of her eyes.

"Do you mind if I read some of your mother's diary?"

he asked gently, as if he expected her to suddenly go ballistic.

"Since we both need answers, be my guest."

He read passages out loud skimming the pages she'd just read until he suddenly paused then started flipping back to an earlier passage. He read fast, saying words over and over again, until they started making sense.

"What is it?" She moved closer to try and look over his shoulder.

"I think I've found a code in your mother's journal," he said.

"Don't be ridiculous, my mother wouldn't put a code in her personal journal. Why would she do that?"

Excitement suddenly glistened behind Sloan's dark brown irises. "Don't you see? A normal mother wouldn't, but a woman who knew the whereabouts of a priceless treasure might."

Breath caught in her throat. It couldn't be true. Could it? She felt dizzy for a moment. Disoriented. Like her life was spinning out of control. She pressed her lips together and swallowed the lump that threatened to rise.

He squeezed her shoulder and it grounded her somehow. Gave her a little more strength. "You can handle this, Raven. You're stronger than you think."

She liked the way he said those words. As if he really believed in her. It'd been a long time since anyone had. "If you think you've found a secret code, what does it say?"

Almost excited, he flipped back to the beginning of the journal, he said, "Look here." One finger pointed at a word. "See how your mother's handwriting is different here. It's a simple code, but effective."

Raven squinted at the page. She hadn't noticed previously, but now that he pointed it out it jumped out at her. "You mean the way she tilts one word to the left rather than the right?"

"Definitely," he said and started flipping the pages

again. Every third page has a word that's the same way."

He flipped pages again. Page 1, page 3, page 6. "On... an... island."

She froze. "On an island? Not that island again."

"I'll read it, you listen, see if it means anything to you," he said.

"Okay."

"On an island, in... an... ocean... lies... a... castle... Heart's Devotion."

They looked at each other with excitement at that part. "This is it," he said. "The key."

"Keep reading," Raven squeezed her knees up to her chest and waited.

King... and... Queen... and... Golden... Princess..." He glanced at her. Let his gaze sweep over her long blond hair.

"It's amazing how she planted those words into the story without making them stand out, except for the angle of her script," Raven said.

He nodded agreement then flipped through more of the pages. *"Behold... their... realm... with... guarded... interest."* He paused then said them out loud a few times. "Any ideas about that part?"

She shook her head. "Maybe, since they're guarding something."

He grinned and agreed. "This is definitely it!" Then he continued. *"Across... the... sea... beyond... the... wall..."*

She listened intently. The last part didn't make much sense either. "Is that all there is?"

He flipped further. "There's more. *'a... name... that... doesn't...suit... at... all...*

Pages flipped quickly between his words.

The...key... becomes... for... those... who... seek... the... answer... to... its... own... mystique."

She let the words sink in. He read them again, quickly turning the pages in between to make the transition of the words as smooth as possible.

"In the journal, my mother called me a princess, and said the house on the island was their castle!" Her heart rate picked up.

He grinned at her.

The smile wiped off her face. "You mean this is what you've been looking for? What Barry wanted so badly?"

He grabbed her shoulders and kissed her forehead. She felt like she was twelve again. Only, she really hated that the big, tough guy was kissing her forehead and not her mouth.

"I can't believe we found it. That we managed to get what the others couldn't find. What Barry tried to kill me for," she said in a whisper.

"We definitely couldn't have found this clue without you." He paused. "At least not in the time given by Brimm."

"What does it all mean?"

"It means we have to go back."

She already knew that but didn't want to admit it to herself. She closed her eyes. "To the island."

"You don't have to come with me, Raven. I'll have someone protect you while I'm gone. You won't be alone."

How many people did he know who'd put their lives on the line for her? Johnson had protected her, and look what happened to him. For all of about two seconds, she considered staying here and letting Sloan go back alone. But in reality there was no way she'd let him search that house without her. It was her island! It was her family's responsibility. She wanted to be the one who found it. And, more than that, she wanted to remember her summers there.

His tough exterior and beautiful eyes had nothing to do

with her decision, nothing at all.

"I'm going with you," she said. "I need to."

He hesitated. Was he going to say no?

"Good. I may need your help when we get there especially if biometrics have been set up there, too. It's just as likely they have similar security on the island."

Raven frowned. Her stomach churned again. "But I don't remember the island. So if there's a secret room it won't be quite as easy to find as it was here in Uncle Phil's house."

He patted her hand then threaded his long fingers through hers. She liked the way he could make her feel again. She'd been numb for far too long.

"Maybe things will start to come back when we get close to finding the solution."

Maybe she'd find out the hard way. She thought about Barry trying to kill her and hated to consider the possibility that Sloan might have the same thing in store for her.

CHAPTER TWELVE

A DAY later they made for the island in Sloan's boat, which they'd found undamaged on the beach. It wasn't long before they motored toward the dock on the far side of the island. Salt air tingled in her nostrils and she could practically taste the tang. Her newfound bravado suddenly had a newfound fragility.

She stared at the old house as they approached it from the cliff. This time she saw the plaque over the door when they entered. "Heart's Devotion." And, she noted the faded red roses framing the gilded Gothic style of writing. Staring at the façade, she tried to remember what it might have looked like in better days. Maybe freshly painted.

"I can't believe this place is mine and I can't remember one second of it. It's been eight years since my parents died and my uncle never mentioned this place, why?"

Sloan scrunched his shoulders up. His hands hung from his pockets by his thumbs. "I have the feeling before this is over you'll have those answers. Right now, all I can say is take it a day at a time. If it's meant to be, the memories will come back."

"I don't know if they will or not. After seeing words as clear as day in my mother's journal about a life I don't remember, it makes me think there's something wrong with me. What possible reason would I have to block out such a huge part of my upbringing?"

Sloan's gaze settled on her. "We guard ourselves in many ways, Raven. This may be a form of self-protection for you."

She gasped. "You mean you think I've blocked it from

my memory subconsciously because of something I don't want to remember?"

Suddenly he looked concerned. "Uh... no... I don't know. Look, let's just look around, see if anything rings a bell."

There was no doubt he was trying to get away from that topic, and fast. And it was becoming suddenly very clear that the issue made him uncomfortable. That made her angry. He wasn't telling her everything. Her shoulders wilted, but only for a second because she'd figure this out one way or another.

After wandering the first floor with Sloan close behind her and finding nothing, she pressed her fingers to her temples and closed her eyes. She tried to concentrate but all she got was a whopper of a headache. "Nothing. There is nothing in this house that I remember."

"Doesn't matter. We have the riddle. We can use it to help us find the secret. Hopefully before Brimm finds us, again."

"On an island, in an ocean, lies a castle..." she said in a rhyming voice. "This isn't exactly a castle. But my mother called it a castle in her diary, so a castle it is."

He gave her one of those looks that made her think he knew more than she did. She was getting really tired of that.

"Just spit it out, Brockway! What the hell is it you aren't telling me?"

His tough exterior didn't fool her. He used those bad boy good looks to his advantage whenever possible. The hurt expression he'd pasted on didn't work one little bit.

"I'm aware that you don't trust me, Delacoeur," he said using her maiden name the way she had used his. "But do you have to constantly think I'm holding back."

"Yes. Because you are." She stalked away from him. "Did you check the whole house during your time here?"

"Inside and out. I haven't found a thing," he said, reaching into his pocket to dig out the journal he'd been carrying for her. "What's the next line, again?" he mumbled to himself.

"King and Queen and Golden Princess," she said without even thinking about it.

"How'd you remember that already?"

She turned to him, still frowning. "I don't know how, but now that I've heard it, I seem to remember it and in my mind it has a tune."

Sloan slapped his hands together. "I bet your parents taught it to you as a child's song, or a nursery rhyme in case something happened to the diary. What better way, to make sure you never lose it?

What he'd just said sparked a growing sense of excitement. "Yes, that's it. It was a nursery rhyme."

"Okay! Some of it makes sense. You're the golden princess. Your parents were the King and Queen, and this was their castle. They probably loved this place."

Not a single ghost of her past haunted her here. "Why don't I remember it then?" She marched towards the living room and stared at the furniture and the fireplace.

He held up a finger, "But the poem said, 'The King and Queen and Golden Princess behold their realm with guarded interest." He raised his hands and indicated the room. The house. "Don't you see? Their job was to guard the ancient treasures that were charged to them. That's the clue that proves the relics have to be here."

"Unless I'm not the golden princess," she said blandly.

He leaned closer, picked up the ends of her hair and rubbed the silken strands in his fingers. "I'd bet my life on the fact that you are."

This couldn't be happening. If this house belonged to her parents and they taught her that poem, why didn't she remember being here? It was one thing to forget a child's verse, but forgetting big chunks of her life, something else altogether.

Sloan's hand slipped away from her hair. "Okay, the next verse. Across the sea, beyond the wall, a name that doesn't suit at all."

"What does that mean?"

"Other than the island is across a sea, I have no idea."

"Me either."

He flipped the pages of the journal again. "The key becomes for those who seek, the answer to its own mystique." He read the poem again under his breath, while Raven recited it out loud.

Each time she said it, she felt a little happier. "The poem is so clear in my head now. How could I have ever forgotten it?"

Sloan thumbed through the pages of the diary again.

"What are you looking for?"

"Maybe there's another clue. Something to tell us where to find the items they protected."

Raven closed her eyes and concentrated on her olfactory senses. She'd heard scents could enhance memories. Connect to them. "Why don't we go through the whole house again?" she said. "Something might strike a chord."

She wandered from room to room, staring at everything as if it should mean something to her, the whole time trailing her fingers across walls looking for buttons to secret doors. After an hour of finding absolutely nothing, her spirits sank again.

If she'd been here before, nothing was coming back except slight pings at certain scents.

Another thought struck. What about that strange man in the fog? What was it he'd said? Something about this being her quest? Did that mean he knew something about the house too? Did he also know more about her life than she did?

Damn it!

Sloan had wandered off on his own search while Raven finished scouting the second floor. This time, not only did she look for a secret door but she also looked at pieces of furniture, pictures, rugs—anything that might pluck a memory for her. Nothing struck a bell.

Finding nothing upstairs, she made her way down to the kitchen. She could barely swallow after inhaling all that dust. Until then she'd almost forgotten about her sore throat. The bruises were turning green and yellow now. The instant she stepped into the kitchen she spotted the basement door. Of course!

After opening the door and flicking on the light switch illuminating the bare light bulb below, a cool, damp, musty smell wafted up to her nostrils. Déjà vu swamped her. That scent—that musty scent, it was something she remembered!

When she moved off the last step onto the mud floor her heart sank, there was nothing here but stone and mortar walls and a few old items, a turnip slicer, an ancient milk churn. Wait, was it her imagination or did the basement seemed bigger than the house above?

There were old studded partitions down here, but no interior walls. Some sections harbored stored items like bundles of shingles leftover from an old roofing project. In the last room she saw a child's bicycle with faded ribbons and a rusted bell on the handlebars. The seat had obviously been pink and white leather, but it had faded with age. She ran her hand over the handlebars, then rang the bell. Time hadn't affected the jingling sound the bell made. The sound reverberated through the basement, then through her mind.

Ripples of nervous sensation took off in her chest. This bicycle had been hers. She remembered the sound of the bell and somewhere in the deepest recesses of her memory, she remembered riding the bike on a narrow dirt path bracketed by stone walls. She'd ridden this little bike in the basement? Why not outside?

With a shiver, she backed away from the bicycle. How could she remember a darned bell, and very little else?

She went to the outer wall and leaned against the cool stone. She needed something solid to ground her. The rough, damp texture of the stone against her bare arm instantly spiked another fragment of memory. A flash so quick, she couldn't catch it. But there had been another memory, however fleeting.

Looking back at the stairs, she guessed at where the basement should end in correlation to the house above. This section of basement had to have been built underground since it extended beyond the walls of the upper structure. Maybe the house had been bigger in its heyday?

The floor had a slight slope downward.

She went to the wall at the far end of the underground section and pressed her hand against the rough textured stone to try to elicit another memory.

Nothing happened.

With Uncle Phil's secret room in mind, butterflies circled the pit of her stomach. Could it be? Could the room be here?

She pressed stones and looked for cracks in the mortar, anything that might serve as a latch or a door. It had to be here, it just had to. She ran her fingers over every inch of the wall until her fingertips were nearly raw.

A scuffling noise in a shadowy corner made her breath quicken. There might be rats down here in this old basement. She hated rats.

Unexpectedly, pain detonated at the back of her head initiating an explosion of stars, then a sense of falling into blackness.

* * * * *

Sloan checked his watch and wondered where Raven had gone. He'd given her time alone to try to come to terms with the fact that she owned this house. She had a history here that she didn't remember and that fact obviously bothered her more than the rest of the news he'd thrown at her.

Unfortunately, he understood completely why she didn't remember. When she was a teenager she'd been through horrors no teen should ever experience. The official prognosis had been hysterical amnesia, all because of Sloan's cousin, Victor, Barry's older brother.

The bastard had capsized Raven's parents' boat out in the ocean, too far offshore for anyone to swim to safety. The Protectorate assumed they'd have survived for quite a while before the cold made them unable to tread water any longer. Raven had been the only one with a lifejacket. Thank God she'd been found before hypothermia had set in, but not before she'd seen her parents drown. At least that was the theory. They hadn't been able to ask any questions, since she'd been unable to remember.

Imagine how she'd feel if she knew Victor killed her parents, then she married his brother Barry. If the idiot hadn't died in the process of trying to kill her, Sloan might have helped him along.

He'd never be able to make up for what his relatives did to her. Worse, when she learned the truth, she'd hate him, too. He rubbed his chest over his heart and felt that same old ache that had been there for way too long.

Maybe he hoped she'd never remember because she'd suffer those horrors all over again. He hated that he'd brought her back here and that he might be the cause of her remembering those horrors. Maybe he *was* a worse bastard than his relatives because without this interference she might've found peace eventually.

He glanced at his watch again. It was late and she must be hungry. They'd only grabbed a quick coffee and muffin on the ferry.

"Raven," he called.

She didn't answer. He jogged up the stairs and did a quick search, then thumped back downstairs and looked around. When he reached the kitchen he found the basement door ajar.

"Raven, you down there?" he shouter a little louder, his voice could resonate when he wanted it to. "Raven..." So why hadn't she answered? He stomped down the basement stairs and quickly scanned the room.

Where was she?

Just as he turned to go back upstairs he spotted her crumpled form on the ground near the far wall, almost hidden by pile of old junk. He raced across the basement. "Raven!"

She lay so still, he choked out a spate of curses while he dropped to the ground and felt for a pulse. Thank God, it was strong. Releasing a long breath, he gently nudged her arm. She moaned and started to come around.

"Raven. Raven. Wake up. Did you faint?"

She moaned again and moved a little. One hand went up to touch the side of her head. "I think someone hit me."

He checked where her fingers were touching and found a nasty looking red lump. She had indeed been knocked out. He looked at the marks in the dirt. She'd also been dragged to this dark corner. "Do you remember being moved?"

Her eyes opened slowly and she winced. "Yes, I think so. Someone grabbed me under the arms and yanked me along the floor before I blacked out."

"Damn it! I shouldn't have left you alone."

"How could you know what was going to happen?"

"I should have considered that Brimm's men might

still be here. Or at the very least, the possibility that they might come back."

"But if it was them, why'd they leave me?" she asked rubbing her head and trying to sit up.

"At this point, who the hell knows? They're not doing things logically as far as I can tell. And, why would they drag you over here?" To hide her from being found? "It doesn't seem like Brimm's style to me. He'd attack openly and I don't think he'd hide you."

"I think I can get up now." She pushed up enough to lean on her elbows before he helped her sit up the rest of the way. It took a moment or two to regain her equilibrium before he helped her stand. He didn't let go while she tested her legs.

The light fragrance in her hair tantalized him. He ached to kiss the base of her neck and under her earlobes. Damn it, he had get over her, she'd never be able to forgive him when she learned the truth.

She extricated herself from his hands. "I'm okay. My head's feeling better." Obviously not true, but she had that Delacoeur spirit, she wasn't ready to give up yet.

"Wait a minute! Look at that." He pointed at a footprint in the dirt that led straight through the wall. When he looked closer, the heel mark butted right up against the stone. The rest of the shoe print had to be on the other side.

"You found it! There's got to be a secret door here," Raven said. "I looked for ages, but couldn't find anything. Then I got clunked on the noggin."

"Maybe because you were getting too close for comfort?" Sloan started pressing and prodding at the wall. "And look here, there are several strange scraping marks in the dirt, too. In an arc, just the way a door would make when it swung open. But it's solid stone."

"That mark wasn't there before I was knocked out, I'd swear to it," she said.

He tapped the stone in front of the arc in the dirt. It sounded hollow.

"Maybe." She stared at the wall then the marks in the dirt and wondered why they'd drag her from the place she'd been attacked. "Maybe he was going to drag me inside but you stopped him by coming down here before he could pull me through."

He cursed. "I think you're right. It's a damned good thing I came down here when I did."

He put an arm around her shoulder and she sagged against him. "I think you saved me again."

"I think we've found your parents' secret room," he said, giving her a sympathetic squeeze. "It seems the room is not so secret, though, if someone else is using it. We might already be too late."

"And, whoever hit me is behind that wall."

"I'm going to make him sorry for what he did to you, the bastard!" He let go of her shoulders and molded a hand over hers. "Let's see if we can find the opening mechanism. Once we find it you get out of the way, okay? I have a bone to pick with your attacker."

Raven smiled. "I'd actually like to see you kick his ass."

Sloan laughed. "I like this new Raven."

"You might have created a monster," she said. He could hear the first hint of humor in her voice. Oh, he wanted to know that side of her again. She had no idea.

CHAPTER THIRTEEN

"MONSTER OR not, maybe you probably should go upstairs and put some ice on that lump on your head. Besides, it could be dangerous in there."

She held up a hand. "We've been through hell for this secret door, Johnson even got shot. I'm not leaving now that we've finally found it."

He glanced at the lump on her head. True, she was most likely sporting a killer headache, but apparently she had a hard head and an even more desperate need to learn the truth.

"I'm staying," she said.

"Damn it, woman, you're the most stubborn person I've ever met." Sloan hoped to hell that whoever knocked her out hadn't already found the artifacts. How'd they figured out the secret door?

"Thanks," she said as if it had been a compliment. "Looks like we have something in common, then," she said in a firm voice. 'Let's get to work, we need to find out how to get inside."

Sloan turned and started pushing each stone in succession just like Raven had done before she'd been knocked out. She knew that method wouldn't work.

Finally, he stopped and heaved an exasperated sigh.

Knowing her answer was on the other side of that wall she backed up to get a broader perspective. She backed a few steps too far and shrieked when she felt a sticky web caught in her hair. Silky strands trailed across her ear sending chills down her spine. Bending over and fluffing her hair to get rid of any possible spiders, she ignored the pain in her head. She'd survive the pain, but couldn't abide the thought of spiders in her hair.

Sloan's deep rumble of laughter caught her by surprise. Still bent over and brushing bits of web out of her hair, she tipped her head sideways and frowned at him.

Her actions simply made him laugh harder. Imagining the scene from his perspective, she had to grin.

Meanwhile, the strange little poem had been repeating in her head. She started saying it out loud again.

"On an island, in an ocean, lies a castle, Heart's Devotion.

King and Queen and Golden Princess, Behold their realm with guarded interest

Across the sea, beyond the wall! "Beyond the wall! It's part of the poem! This is the wall. We're getting closer I can feel it," she said from her bent-over position.

He stopped laughing instantly and started searching through the rafters over the stone to see if there was a latch. A smudge of dirt marked his cheek when he climbed back down. Better than spiders in his hair.

Feeling a little woozy, she sat down while he looked.

"Why can't we find a way in?" He said, glancing back at her and frowning when he realized she was on the ground. "Raven! You're not feeling well. We should get you out of here."

She agreed in spirit that sitting on this dank earth was making her feel chilled. And she could use something for the headache, a couple of pain relievers would do the trick, but hades would freeze over before she'd leave here when they were so close. She swiped at her hair and tipped her head sideways again to evict any leftover spiders. She'd probably continue to do that until she got it washed. Suddenly, at the base of one of the stones she caught a tiny glint of metal. So small it looked like a nail that had broken off and had stuck to the mortar when the stones were laid.

"There's something down there," she said getting on her knees near Sloan's foot.

He leaned over and looked where she was pointing. "You found it! It probably activates like this... He toed the latch and they both moved out of the way while the stone silently opened outward.

Casting an urgent warning glance at Raven to be quiet, he stepped inside the dark opening.

She followed closely behind him, the dull, throbbing pain in her head all but forgotten.

They weren't in a room, but a tunnel. Leading where?

Sloan reached up to a shelf inside the door and grabbed an oil lantern, rummaged in his shirt pocket and pulled out a lighter. He lit the lantern and the narrow passageway illuminated. No attackers hid in the hall but a long stone hallway sloped down and disappeared into the dark maw ahead.

It was a familiar hall, possibly the path on which she'd ridden her bike.

Sloan led the way.

Solid rock walls and more dirt floor wound around and down until it opened into a cavern. The island must have a huge cave system underground. She thought of the cave where Sloan tied up his boat and wondered if the caves linked together. If so, this route would certainly be preferable to climbing down the side of the cliff face to get to the boat.

"Be careful! Whoever hit me might still be here," she said. Not that Sloan needed the warning.

"Just stay near me, Raven. Don't wander off."

Roots grew through the ceiling, long fibers and strands hung down like old witch's hair. Another memory pinged. Had she thought that as a child?

In the center of the cavern there were several oversized boulders positioned in a circle. Most likely a deliberate layout, it reminded her of a mini Stonehenge.

Sloan whistled. "This isn't huge, but I imagine it would have held quite a bit of rum in its day."

She made a face. "Great, my claim to fame is that my family tree consists of rum running treasure hunters?"

Sloan held up the lantern to illuminate as much of the room as possible. "It looks like there are several passages leading out of here. I'm guessing whoever hit you is long gone. By the look of the passages going off in all directions, we're going to have to do some big-time surveillance down here."

She wavered and pressed one hand against a wall to steady herself. Had the ground moved, or was she dizzy? Suddenly, the pain in her head started to feel like a thudding weight on her brain. She cringed and pressed two fingers over her left eye.

"But not today," he said. We're getting out of here." He must've noticed her actions.

She didn't argue this time. They backtracked to the basement where Sloan flipped the latch with his toe and they watched the door close, its edges so perfectly carved, the wall fit together without any indication of a door even when they knew it was there.

"What's the plan for tonight?" she asked.

"You take painkillers and get some sleep while I stay on guard. Even if I could call for backup, it'd take hours for Protectorate members to get here. Besides, I'm not ready to give up yet. We're so close. We can solve this thing together."

She should be more afraid. There shouldn't be a tingle of excitement shooting up her spine right now. She shouldn't trust Sloan so implicitly, but she did. He'd keep them both safe tonight.

She nodded and said, "We'll find it."

* * * * *

Sloan cursed himself for wanting to hold her tight in his arms right now. Until she knew the whole truth about his heritage, he had to back off.

Of course she needed to know about him, eventually, but not until they found the relics and she learned the truth of her heritage. "Why don't you lie down until your headache is gone?"

"I think you're right this time," she said. She was pale, and didn't demand they keep going.

"Have a nap. When you wake up you might feel better."

"I thought you weren't supposed to sleep after a thump on the head?"

"I'll make sure you're okay," he said. "The sofa should be comfortable enough and I'll be in the kitchen next door getting dinner ready, that way, I can keep an eye on you. I'll wake you and check on you, if you sleep too long."

When they climbed the stairs and got to the kitchen, she went directly to the sofa and kicked off her shoes, stuffing the sofa cushion under her head and stretching out.

He brought her a glass of water and some painkillers.

"Thanks," she said, swallowing them down gratefully and closing her eyes against the pain.

While she managed to drift off, he noted the dark shadows smudging the soft tissue under her eyes. The muscles in his jaw tightened. This shouldn't have happened on his watch.

With the recent knowledge that the Delacoeurs had a penchant for secret rooms, he wondered if Raven might be at risk in this room, too. Did it have secret doors? He'd already made sure the walls were covered in old plaster and paint even so, he walked the circumference of the living room again.

CHAPTER FOURTEEN

THE SENSATION of falling jerked Raven awake from a recurring bad dream. Realizing where she was, she brushed hair out of her eyes and touched the bump on her head. Ouch. She'd probably be sore for a day or two thanks to her attacker. At least the pain pills had worked and her headache was gone. Heck, even her throat felt better.

She rolled onto her back and stretched. A delicious odor wafted into the room. Her stomach gurgled and reminded her how hungry she was. She got up and she made for the kitchen.

Sloan was frying steaks in a cast iron frying pan. Vegetables simmered on the back burner.

"That smells so good," she said.

"Hi." He looked her over with concern. "How's the head?"

"Better."

"What woke you?" He turned one of the steaks over and it sizzled in the pan.

"Probably the aroma of food." She ran a hand over her stomach. She didn't want to mention the bad dream.

Steak and equally tasty looking mushrooms and onions sizzling in the pan made her mouth water.

"I found the meat in the freezer this morning. I thought Brimm and his men had eaten everything, but lucky for us they missed the upright freezer. And since we managed to get milk and eggs at the convenience store on our way here, we'll be good to go for a few days."

She sat down and flattened her hands on the table in front of her. "Sloan, have you decided what you want to do about the caves?" she asked, glancing out the kitchen window.   It was dark outside now and the thought of crawling around underground at night, even though it was continuously dark down there, didn't appeal to her.

He picked up a coffee mug beside the stove and downed the last of its contents then carried their plates to the table and sat opposite her. "I think we should wait and check it out in the morning." He waited for her to cut her steak and take a bite.

She groaned in pleasure. "Maybe we should look tonight? Someone's already down there. What if they're plundering the artifacts while we're sitting here eating our meal?"

"Plundering?" He grinned. "I've been thinking about that, I have the feeling no one is going to get into anything unless they have your fingerprint. We have an advantage they don't."

"The poem led us to that wall."

"And the next part isn't going to be as easy as beyond the wall."

She recited the complete poem out loud until she got to the second last verse. "A name that doesn't suit at all? What could that mean?"

He put his fork down and rubbed the back of his neck. "You've got me. I've been going over that riddle all day and I can't figure it out."

"Heart's Devotion." She chewed on a bite of the melt-in-her-mouth steak. "Yum, this is good," she said. "What if it's not the name of the house but the caves? Could they be the heart of the island?"

He shrugged but looked instantly interested. "Maybe."

She took another bite of steak. He'd nearly finished his meal while she'd been pondering the poem. He waited for her to finish and they put the dishes in the sink to soak and went back to the living room.

"How long do you think we have before Brimm comes looking for us again?"

Sloan's expression tightened. "Wish I knew. Now that Johnson's bedridden, I don't have my Chicago connection. That leaves us more vulnerable."

Raven stared at Sloan. What wasn't he telling her? Why were they more vulnerable without Johnson? Didn't he work for The Protectorate? Or maybe he didn't completely trust them either.

"Speaking of Johnson, I called him and had a chat while you were sleeping. He'll be in the hospital for a while but he's going to recover completely according to the doc."

"I'm so glad."

"Me too, he's a good man."

Her head tingled. "My head is still crawling, I'm sure there's a nest of spiders in there," she said with a grin.

He leaned over and parted her hair gently to search for the non-existent arachnids. He spent a few seconds looking at her bump. "That's a nasty lump. I guess you must have a hard head, too, since you seem to be doing pretty well. Not seeing double or anything, are you?"

"No, but if I lean over, I feel my heart pounding in my head."

"If I were a doctor, know what I'd say?"

She noted the twinkle in his eyes.

They both spoke in unison. "Don't bend over."

He looked at his watch. "It's getting late, we should grab some shuteye."

"With people possibly lurking in the house?" She already imagined threatening shadows growing in the corners of the room thanks to her vivid imagination.

"We'll stick together," he said. "It might be better to stay right here in front of the fire, tonight."

As soon as he said it, she heard a foghorn in the distance. It would be a cool night. She looked around. "But there's only one sofa."

"I'll pull the settee in from the other room," he said. "I can sleep on the floor if you'd rather have the sofa."

"The settee is fine, just the right length for me and we both need some sleep to be fresh for our search tomorrow."

After he pulled the antique settee into the room, he went upstairs for pillows and blankets. While he was gone, she moved to the footstool near the fireplace where she could grab a poker for a weapon if she needed one. He probably still had the gun from her uncle's house, or did he? Had he been able to get it through customs?

Either way, she felt safer when he returned with the bedding, though she didn't admit it to him. She happily prodded the cushions of the settee, glad to see it was going to be quite comfortable. She plumped the pillow, snuggled under the soft blanket he'd given her and watched him preparing the sofa for himself.

The fire flickered, casting soft light around the room. Though he kept his gaze off her, she noticed he didn't try to close his eyes and sleep. She doubted he'd even try until he was sure they were safe.

"We can start searching the caves again in the morning," she said.

"My thoughts exactly," he said, folding his arms over his chest and staring at the ceiling.

As creepy as it was down there in the cave, solving the puzzle and finding the missing artifact was beginning to get under her skin. Who knew what they'd find tomorrow?

"Since you seem to have a knack for finding hidden doors and secret rooms, I'm hoping we'll find something tomorrow," he said.

"No pressure though, right?" She grinned at him and noted he'd glanced at her quickly and looked relieved when he saw she'd been joking. It wasn't until then she realized he was walking on eggshells around her. Or was that her imagination?

"Absolutely pressure." He smiled. He had a nice face

when he smiled. "I expect with your guidance and I'm sure we'll find something down there."

"Good thing I'm getting to know you. I'm actually starting to feel safe right now," she said.

"I'm glad you trust me," he said, not meeting her gaze.

"I wouldn't go quite that far."

CHAPTER FIFTEEN

SLOAN SLEPT with one eye open. He always slept lightly, but tonight he was on high alert. Luckily, he could catnap enough to be able to function tomorrow. He didn't want to scare Raven, but they couldn't be in a more dangerous situation than they were right now. Stranded on this island with someone who knew the passageways in the old house left them very vulnerable.

And right now Raven looked like hell warmed up. Her face had been so pale after that crack on the noggin, he was afraid she might have a concussion. She needed a good night's sleep.

The best he could do—stay on guard and try to figure this thing out. Was he doing the right thing keeping so many secrets from her? She obviously desperately wanted to know about her past.

Sometime during the night he decided it would be better to tell her the truth, or as much as he dared tell her without bringing it all back in a torrent. Last thing he wanted was to cause her to relapse and withdraw into herself again. Then again, knowing the truth might mean she'd never trust him again.

He just couldn't keep leading her down this path unaware of what she was walking into and with whom. If he did, he'd be no better than Barry.

Waiting to talk to her left him negatively charged. At least when she woke just after dawn, he could tell she was feeling better and ready to take on the world and find the treasure. Meanwhile, he didn't eat much at breakfast.

After washing up, she found him staring out the window. "Are you ready to go?"

He swallowed hard. "Raven, before we go any further I have to tell you something." Was he doing the right thing by telling her the truth? Would it bring back all her horrific memories of the drowning? "I have something very important to tell you and I hope you understand I'm telling you this because I want you to be able to trust me."

She reached out and touched his hand. "What is it, Sloan?"

He'd judge her reaction by how fast she pulled her hand away when he told her. "It was my cousin, Victor Brockway, who killed your parents."

She laughed but instantly sounded nervous. He'd been telling her they'd been killed, but he wasn't sure she really believed it.

"My parents drowned in a boating accident," she said, proving his theory. She didn't' believe him.

"Yes, they did drown, but Victor caused the boat to sink. He killed them to get their hidden treasure. The treasure your family has been protecting for centuries." Sloan clenched his hands at his sides. "Victor was obviously a sociopathic delusional who should have been put away, but no one knew how bad he was until it happened."

Her face turned white so fast he thought she might be having a relapse of head trauma. He lurched toward her but she shrank away.

Hell, maybe he should have told her this in Chicago where he could get her to a hospital if she went into shock. After all, she had some major psychological blockages from the horrors of seeing her parents die, otherwise she wouldn't have blocked out her memories for so long.

Her blue-eyed stare sliced him to the core.

"Are you saying my parents were killed for whatever you're looking for right now? By your relative?"

Oh crap! He'd done the wrong thing. He'd put a wedge

between them that could never be removed. When she found out her husband had also been a Brockway and not a Gale, it would be ten times worse.

* * * * *

Raven felt ice form in her veins. Was she forever going to be a gullible idiot? She couldn't believe she'd almost trusted this guy. He was nothing but a cold-hearted, cold-blooded treasure hunter who was related to the man who killed her parents. What possible reason did he have for telling her this now? To scare her?

"Where is Victor, now?" she asked. "Why isn't he hounding me for the treasure instead of you? I'm assuming he killed my parents then realized he couldn't find the artifact anyway, since we're still looking for it."

Sloan grimaced. "Victor disappeared after your family died. When The Protectorate found out about his evil plot, they abhorred and condemned what he did, and rightfully so. They shut out everyone in the family as a result."

"Including you?"

"Until just recently, yes." He looked shamed.

She wanted to slap him but didn't know if she'd be able to stop if she started. She held her anger in, no sense giving him the satisfaction of the reaction he expected, and after all, according to him she'd been doing that for years in the form of amnesia. "Why'd the Protectorate let you back?"

"Because of Barry. I look enough like him to get information from the hoods he'd been dealing with. AKA Jason Brimm."

"Until Victor's heinous crime, my side of the family had been members of The Protectorate as long as your family—in fact, our families worked together."

His hands were fisted. His signet ring sparkled viciously in the morning light. She had to look away. This man who'd lied to her since day one wanted her to trust him while his own cousin had taken everything she held dear.

She turned to escape. If he touched her right now she'd scream. Just being in the same room with him made her skin crawl.

He cleared his throat but didn't look at her. "The betrayal was the worst possible thing Victor could do to my family, Raven. Honor was our creed. He wiped out centuries of self-sacrifice in one avaricious-murderous moment. You have no idea how this has affected my family's name. "

"Pardon me if I have no sympathy for your family's loss of credibility. At least you have a family," she ground out, hate spilling from every pore. She didn't care. He deserved her revulsion. She swallowed the lump that threatened to choke her. Somewhere in the back of her mind she remembered he didn't have parents either. Both of his parents had died horribly as well. She couldn't care about that right now, her heart was too raw and pained for her own family.

His ragged expression nearly changed her mind; he looked so devastated right now. She had to force herself to believe it was all an act.

"I understand how you must feel," he began, starting to follow her.

"Go away and leave me alone. I don't want to look at you right now. Or ever again." Her throat was so tight her voice had become hoarse again.

"I can't go away, because if I leave I'll be no better than Victor. I intend to carry on and expunge my father's name. I will protect you from Brimm and whoever else thinks they might benefit from your death in the meantime, and I'll help you find answers."

She let a disgusted sound escape from her throat.

"Why did you tell me this? Did you think I could ever in a million years forgive you? Did you think if you promised to protect me, to save my life, that all would be forgotten?" Damn it, she was doing everything in her power to stop tears from pouring down her cheeks, she couldn't let that happen. Not in front of *him*.

Worse. She'd been attracted to him – unbelievable! Caring for him would have been worse than marrying Barry. She sank onto the sofa and stared at the hardwood floor.

Lethargy seeped into her bones. Despair threatened to swamp her while she felt the loss of her parents all over again. Only this time, it was even harder to contemplate the probability that her parents had been murdered by Sloan's cousin and yet, he'd been brazen enough to let her know he wanted exactly what Barry had wanted. The treasure.

She eyed his expensive watch. A hefty paycheck must come with the job. Her parents never lacked in funds, either. How awful their betrayal must've been when they realized it was at the hands of a member of their own group.

Raven grabbed the sofa cushion and squeezed it in front of her while she curled up into a ball. She felt alone—so—so—alone.

Again.

CHAPTER SIXTEEN

EVEN WORSE, Sloan had to know how much she'd hate him for this. How she'd blame him for using her just like his cousin had done. And worse, the horrors went all the way back to the death of her parents.

If he was telling her the truth, if it had been the truth all along, it made sense that her parents had insisted she train in many forms of self-preservation such as martial arts, fencing, deep woods survival, use of weapons on the firing range. It might be possible they wanted her to be initiated into The Protectorate, to carry on the honor of her family name when she was old enough. Too bad she'd never done any training, she needed protection—because she could trust no one!

For all intents and purposes, she was trapped on this island, but for a different reason this time. One thing inside her had changed, though, she wasn't giving up. She wouldn't leave here until she found answers—about her parents, their deaths and about the treasure her mother had written about in code in her journal. The code had been real, Sloan hadn't lied about that part.

Finding the artifacts somewhere in the caves had become even more urgent.

She glanced around. It surprised her that he'd left her alone after telling her those horrible things. She could see into the kitchen, he was gone. She had no idea where he went and she didn't give a damn, either.

"Beyond the Wall... A name that doesn't suit at all," she said out loud, snatching up a poker and striding toward the basement door. She took a flashlight off the kitchen table on the way by. She'd do this by herself.

The bare bulb in the basement created long shadows that left her edgy after being attacked here the day before. Keeping an eye out so no one could knock her out again, she used the toe of her shoe to click the latch and waited for the wall to open.

It was very dark and exceedingly quiet inside the tunnel when she stepped inside—a harbinger of death? Shivers rushed up her arms—didn't matter, she'd never quit now.

According to her mother's diary, Raven had been on the island many times as a child so she must know her way around. But, had she ever been in the secret room her parents had died for?

She made it through the first cave and wandered around mini Stonehenge. Nothing. Next, she chose one of the three tunnels branching off into the underground labyrinth. Afraid she might get lost, she dragged her heel into the sand every few feet to make an arrow. That way she wouldn't go in circles and she should be able to backtrack to the basement if she got lost.

The flashlight she'd brought wasn't as bright as she would have liked down here in the dark but she pressed on.

Suddenly angry voices erupted ahead of her. It was Sloan's voice—he was already down here—he'd gone without her! His words were muffled so she hurried forward to find out who in hell he was talking to?

She flicked off the flashlight and sneaked along the tunnel. The walls were cool and clammy down here, but not exactly wet. She slid her feet along the ground feeling her way so she wouldn't trip over the larger rocks and pebbles sticking out of the ground.

When muted light appeared ahead, she carved another arrow with her heel then slinked toward the opening to another cavern.

The voices were getting angrier.

At the end of the tunnel, a massive cavern about twice

the size of the one near the house opened before her. The center of the room held several open packing boxes. Raffia had been pulled out and spread around the floor.

Near the crates, two men faced off. She knew Sloan's body shape instantly, even in the poorly lit cave. The other man looked familiar too, but it wasn't who she'd expected to see when she heard the men arguing. Instead of Jason Brimm it was her mysterious friend from the fog? Davey. Except, he looked younger now. His white hair was gone.

Sloan reached up and rubbed the side of his head. "You bastard, where have you been all these years? We thought you were dead." The men had no idea she was watching them from her dark tunnel opening.

"I am dead. Dead to a sniveling family that doesn't have the guts to take what is their due and to hell with that damned Protectorate. I'm taking what's mine. Finder's keepers."

"You're delusional," Sloan grated, staggering slightly.

Sloan shifted sideways and she saw blood dripping off a gash on his arm, most likely caused by the knife in Davey's hand. He'd seemed so nice in the fog—she'd been a gullible idiot yet again!

"You can have the damned treasure, I won't stop you, but I'll kill you before you touch one hair on Raven's head," Sloan said.

Raven dug her fingers into the solid rock and tried to hang on to every word being said. Her heart rate doubled at Sloan's words. He really did care about her. He was protecting her again, and she hadn't been able to appreciate that fact.

"You're a sad excuse of a Brockway," Davey spat out while pointing the knife at Sloan's midsection. "You should've been able to find the goods with the help of that Delacoeur woman. Why haven't you?"

"Don't you mean your sister-in-law?" Sloan said in an angry voice.

Raven's mind couldn't comprehend what he'd just said. She felt fuzzy, out of sink. She must be hearing things. How could this man be her brother-in-law? That would mean that he was Barry's brother. But Barry had no living relatives. A mist of incomprehension settled over her and she tried to force her way out of it.

Sloan winced when he moved his arm up to protect himself from another slashing attack. "Let me see, maybe because she can't remember a thing since her parents were killed right in front of her, but you know all about that don't you, since you're the one who killed them."

After hearing that, she lost her footing on a rock, fell sideways and slammed her shoulder against the wall. It stung like fire but it brought her to her senses. She'd been with her parents when they died?

"What the hell are you talking about," she cried out in an anguished voice when she stepped out of the tunnel. Both men turned in her direction.

Davey's grin found her and turned nasty while Sloan spat out a curse. "Get out of here, Raven, before it's too late."

Without a second's hesitation she dashed back into the tunnel. She'd seen her parents die? She was with them? She rubbed her temples. Her chest tightened to point of barely being able to breathe. She hadn't gone far when she heard a shot.

"Sloan!" she screamed and barely managed to stop short at the opening.

"The first shot missed him, Missy, but the next one won't if you don't come back here." The menace in his voice left no possibility that he was lying to her.

She edged forward, but hung back just far enough to be unseen but still hear what they were saying. "Don't listen to him, Raven, he'll kill us bo...." A thud sounded and

Sloan's voice cut off mid-word.

Raven didn't think—she turned back and lurched through the tunnel opening again where she spotted Sloan sprawled on the ground. Two oversized men entered the room from an opposite tunnel to join Davey who she now knew had to be Victor.

Sloan had been telling her the truth. His cousins were evil and Sloan wasn't like them. He'd proven himself to her in so many ways and she'd been too afraid to let her guard down and trust him. If he died now, she'd never be able to tell him how much she... She thought about the kisses. She couldn't go there right now.

"We're taking him with us, Raven," Victor shouted in that fake old man's voice he'd used on the beach as Davey.

It *was* the old man's voice only he wasn't really that old. He'd been playing her, trying to find out if she knew anything. Her blood boiled.

"You have twenty-four hours to find the treasure or we're going to kill him. He's always been a pain in the ass, anyway," Victor said casting an uncaring glance at Sloan's unconscious body and laughed again. This time the venom in his voice practically burned her flesh. "It's taken me a lot longer than I'd hoped to get my hands on the treasure, but we Brockway men don't give up."

"I wouldn't know about that," she spat at him.

His expression turned vicious. "You should know, you were married to one of us."

"Barry?" She thought her heart was going to burst with the amount of adrenalin pumping through her system. It was true! She wouldn't give Victor the satisfaction of knowing she'd been shocked by the revelation. "He was a bastard."

"That's not a very nice way to talk about my dearly departed brother." Victor snickered. "Not quite as quick on the draw as I'd hoped he'd be. He failed miserably at getting the information we needed, that's why we had to come up with another plan."

Her eyebrows rose. "What do you mean?"

"A little bird leaked information about Jason Brimm to The Protectorate. We knew they'd put Sloan on the job. He's the foremost expert on archaeological digs in this part of the world. Added bonus—he had a crush on you when he was a boy. Hell, you two dated for several months before your parents were whacked. But you don't remember him do you? Or was all of that an act?" Victor laughed again. "Doesn't matter now. His life is in your hands—dumbass has always been a sap for you, and look where it got him." Victor kicked Sloan in the hip.

"Stop it!" Her stomach pitched and for a second she thought she might be sick.

"Does that mean you remember him?" He sounded hopeful.

"No, I don't remember him. I don't believe you, either."

"We knew if we led you to Sloan, he'd do his best to save you and in the interim find the treasure. He'd die for you—will die for you—and you don't even remember him. " Victor laughed. "That's gotta' hurt."

"Oh my Lord." She couldn't believe this was happening. "I honestly don't remember anything about this island or about treasure, I can't help you." Her gaze went to Sloan, her heart breaking at the way she'd treated him.

"I'm betting if the odds get high enough, you'll force yourself to remember. If you want this besotted fool to live, that is." He kicked Sloan's leg this time and Sloan groaned and started to come around.

Victor's two accomplices bent down and grabbed Sloan roughly under the arms. "No time to waste, Victor, Brimm wants this thing over and done with. He's waiting on the Yacht," one of them said.

Victor turned back to Raven before exiting the cavern.

"We'll wait offshore until you come up with the treasure."
He looked at his watch. "You've got one day starting right
now, I suggest you try to remember." He turned and
followed the other men who were carelessly dragging Sloan
away. Sloan moaned and started to struggle. They
knocked him out again.

"Stop it!" she shouted. "I'll tell you right now if
anything happens to Sloan, you'll never get the treasure.
I'll die first."

Victor stopped dead and drilled a cold look at her.
"Where have I heard that before?" He laughed again. "Oh
wait, it was from your parents when they should have been
begging for their lives and look what happened to them."

"You murdering bastard!"

"Sticks and stones, Missy." He turned and waved the
men out ahead of him.

She stood in the cavern watching the men leave. She
was alone and she needed to find the treasure and fast
because Sloan hadn't lied to her, everything he'd told her
had been true.

What a mess. What a convoluted, dangerous mess.
And now Sloan's life was on the line unless she could find
the treasure. Her throat threatened to close. They'd been
searching for months, for years, and they expected her to
find results in one day.

They'd disappeared into the tunnel leaving her behind
to solve the mystery of the missing treasure and somehow
she had to do it to save Sloan's life.

After that last crack to the head, she knew for sure his
life depended on her. She had to find that treasure in
twenty-four hours!

She waited in the dark until she heard a motorboat start
up and motor away. Now, surrounded by darkness and
stone, time was her enemy.

Nausea threatened, but she forced it back with sheer

stubbornness. It'd be easier to go home, to call Johnson and ask him to send for help. She knew where Sloan's boat was secretly moored. She could get away.

But Sloan might die if she did that and would be her fault.

She forced air in and out, in and out. Sloan had risked his life for her in the cave and he'd done it in Chicago.

He loved her.

And she didn't remember him.

After one step she faltered, her knees threatened to buckle. She pressed her hands to her chest. She'd been living her life in denial and suddenly facing the truth had become crucial to staying alive.

She loved him, too!

She loved Sloan Brockway and he was going to die unless she found the relics.

Flipping on the flashlight, she raced to the center of the cave. She ripped through the contents of the packing crates just in case they missed something. The year had been stamped on the wooden slats. Tears pricked at her eyelids at the realization that they'd most likely been here since her parents died.

No surprises, the boxes were empty.

Victor had obviously been searching for years and couldn't find anything.

She slumped to the ground and put her head in her hands. She panicked for about two seconds then forced herself back to her feet to do the unimaginable.

Find that room.

Save Sloan!

CHAPTER SEVENTEEN

TWO HOURS later and totally frustrated, she'd been through every tunnel and every opening she could find. She had even found the hidden boathouse. It made sense that people didn't have to practically repel down a cliff-face to get to the dock, but there hadn't been anything in the form of relics that she could find.

Time was ticking by too fast. She brushed her hair off her face and began to quote the poem out loud again…. *On an island, in an ocean, lies a castle, Heart's Devotion. King and Queen and Golden princess, behold their realm with guarded interest. Across the sea, beyond the wall. A name that doesn't suit at all. The key becomes for those who seek, the answer to its own mystique.*

She groaned. What did it mean? A name that doesn't suit at all.

She found herself back in the cavern with the mini Stonehenge. She tried to make sense of the placement of the stones. There were empty crates here too, left inside the circle. Did that mean anything? She walked the circumference of the boulders, letting her fingers graze along the sides of the rough granite.

Might as well literally walk in circles, she was going in circles anyway.

While she circled the boulders, touching the granite felt real. It somehow helped her to feel grounded. Not so panicky. Why? Why would touching these stones give her a feeling of security, a feeling of familiarity? She searched her addled brain.

Think Raven! There's something about these stones. Somewhere in that maze of blocked memories, images of these stones were trying to surface. In her slowly resurfacing memory, she was much smaller. A child? The boulders were taller than her. She used to run her fingers over the granite. Something on the granite used to make her laugh.

She dropped to her knees, and ran her hands along the granite to try and force the memory fully to the surface. On the first stone, down low, she felt an indentation. Running her fingers over it, she realized it was a turtle.

Excited by her discovery, she moved to the next stone. It was nearly impossible to see the small, carved shape with the naked eye since it was hidden by the rough texture of the granite, she could only find it by touch. This time she found a snake. Each boulder had an animal carved into it. When she got to the fifth boulder, she leaned down and ran her fingers over the carving. It was a bird. She closed her eyes and felt the familiar pattern on the stone. In her mind's eye she could hear a child's tinkling laughter, and a child's rhyme... "On an island...."

It wasn't just a bird. It was a Raven. Just like her name. Was that why she remembered laughing? The Raven had been carved especially for her to amuse her as a child? Were all of the carvings done to keep her occupied while her parents worked?

On her knees, she tried to get a better look. Her long blond hair fell forward and she shoved it behind her ears. A name that doesn't suit at all—Raven! Her hair was blond. It was her name that didn't fit!

This was the clue. The key was a stone! The bird was a Raven.

* * * * *

Pain seared Sloan's shoulder when he was tossed onto the deck of yacht. His hands and feet had been bound, so he couldn't protect his body in the fall. His arm felt a little numb where his cousin Victor had sliced him with the knife; luckily the blade had been dull and hadn't cut as deeply as he'd probably meant to. No risk of losing too much blood, but he could get gangrene from that filthy old knife, if he lived long enough.

None of that mattered. Victor and his goons had left Raven alone in the caves. She must be terrified.

She could run. She knew where the boat was. Dear God, he hoped she had enough sense to make a run for it and not try to save him. No way would these bastards let either of them live, even if she did find what they wanted, which he doubted was possible in the twenty-four hours they'd given her.

Damn it to hell, he couldn't believe his eyes when Victor turned up in the caves. Everyone, including his own family believed Victor had died all those years ago. He'd merely gone underground for years to find the treasure, most likely because he wanted it all for himself.

It gave Sloan some satisfaction when he realized how desperate Victor was right now. He'd found very little information in all that time. He hadn't even found the secret room at Phil's house.

Funny how genes worked, Sloan looked more like his cousin Barry than Victor, but that was as far as it went, he didn't have their lack of morals and greed.

The hired help tossed him under the galley porthole and went inside.

He'd been tied tight enough that his feet and hands were tingling from lack of blood flow. Not good. If he could get loose, he could swim back to the cave and get Raven the hell out, but the odds were slim that he could break free from these knots.

He must've passed out again because he opened his eyes and jerked his head up to see a small helicopter landing on the yacht. Jason Brimm disembarked, but didn't come near Sloan. Every now and then someone checked his ropes, though. The last thug smelled of liquor. They were drinking. If they got as drunk as they had at the house on the island, it might be to his advantage. He couldn't see how many men were on the ship but he could hear their voices in the galley, not clear enough to make out much of what they said, though. He needed to know what they were planning.

It seemed like forever that he'd been working at the ropes trying to get free. His wrists felt like mincemeat. He'd been totally focused on getting himself loose until he heard a voice in the galley that he recognized. More than just familiar, it caused a cold chill to explode across his flesh and drive his blood pressure skyward.

It couldn't be!

Had he gone crazy? He listened again. The man laughed and cursed Sloan down. "You should kill him now, Vic. Why wait for the bitch to turn up?" That voice came across loud and clear.

Raven's fears were real. Barry Gale was alive. Both brothers had pretended to be dead? How the hell had Barry done it? His body had been found at the scene of the accident. Sloan groaned at the realization that the dead man at the accident had gone through the windshield, his facial features had been chewed up by the broken glass. It could have been anyone.

It seemed Raven's intuition had been correct all along. Her supposed dead husband was alive.

Worse, by the sound of things, Barry was getting into the small dingy and heading to the island. Bastard! What was he going to do?

Sloan struggled against the coarse rope and the impossible knots. They were just starting to loosen a little when one of the thugs caught him and clocked him again. Stars, then blackness took over.

* * * * *

Raven pointed the flashlight at her watch again. Four hours had passed with no sign of a secret room. She flopped to the ground and leaned against her stone. If this was the clue, she still had no idea what it meant. She'd tried just about everything she could think of to figure it out, but no luck.

Good thing she'd found a battery operated lantern on the ground where Sloan had been attacked because the batteries in her flashlight were getting low. No way did she want to go back upstairs to find another flashlight. She didn't have time to waste.

"If I've got this information in my head, why can't I access it? Sloan's life depends on it," she said aloud while she brushed grime off her cheek.

Was she wasting her time sitting here trying to figure out the carvings? Should she be looking elsewhere?

Could a brain explode from sheer panic?

Fatigued and feeling as if she'd been climbing and trekking through the caves for hours, she couldn't stop, Sloan's time was running out. Where would she look next? She leaned her head against the rock. Think Raven! Where is it? She knocked her head against the granite in frustration and something under her head moved just a smidge.

She clamored to her hands and knees to look at the raven symbol again. The stone raven shape had depressed ever so slightly. She pushed on it with her hand. It didn't move. She tried one finger even though there was no biometric light.

The raven outline lit up and the familiar sound of gears moving made her clamor out of the way. It wasn't real granite, but it certainly looked and felt real. Now, the artificial stone ground across the floor evoking the musky scents of the earth. She inhaled and another murky memory teased her. It floated through her consciousness like a helium balloon just out of reach.

Meanwhile, the stone had only moved a few inches. The gears must've rusted over the years. She shoved it. With adrenaline pumping and the sheer exhilaration at finding something that could save Sloan, she shoved with all her body weight. The boulder moved another fraction! It actually moved far enough that she could see into the opening beneath it.

Stepping down onto the first wooden step gave her the impetus to shove the rock the rest of the way open. She hoped the wooden steps hadn't rotted. The fact that the gears had rusted didn't give her much faith in the infrastructure below.

Now, she had to go down those wooden steps that led into the dark maw below.

A slow shiver worked across her flesh. It was totally black down there, and she'd need the light. Without taking her foot off that first step, she grabbed the lantern.

What if the rock had a mechanism that would make the trap door close once she got inside and she couldn't get out again? She'd be trapped down there.

She had no choice, she took a couple of tentative steps, testing the strength of the wood. To her relief the bolder overhead stayed open. At least that made her feel a little less claustrophobic while she descended into the hole.

At the bottom, there was nothing but a shallow room, the ceiling so low she could barely stand straight.

Holding up the lantern, she looked around the room. Looking more man-made than natural, carved out of the stone of the island, this small chamber appeared to be empty. It didn't make sense. This was the key that didn't fit at all. Wasn't it?

So where was the treasure?

She scanned the empty room and caught the reflection

of something on the ground. Aiming the light in that direction again, she found a Sterling silver box. Could this be what everyone wanted, a tiny silver box? She expected more. She blew the dirt off the box and looked inside.

Fingers shaking, she extracted a single ring. The metal was thick and a rich golden yellow color with a rough cut stone, definitely not cut by modern lasers. She knew enough about antiquities to realize it was most likely a diamond surrounded by rough-cut rubies. She set the lantern down and put the ring on her thumb. It must have belonged to a man.

Even though the ring was most likely valuable, it could never measure up against the lives of her parents and her uncle. And now Sloan's life hung in the balance…she scanned the small room again. There was nothing else here. This ring was it.

"Thank you, darlin'"" A familiar voice sliced through the silence and caused her heart to gallop recklessly. Barry! The bastard was alive! She pivoted and held the lantern high to see for herself that it was really her husband coming down the stairs.

With a smug look, he held his hand out for the ring while the light in her hand trembled and her mouth went dry.

"I knew you weren't dead," she said finally, in a voice as emotionless as she could devise.

"Well, aren't you the clever little wife. Or are you still technically a widow?" His voice was thick with rancor. "If I'd known you'd be this helpful, I would've brought you here long ago."

"Why did you pretend to be dead?" Her skin crawled. "Who really died? Was there a body in that coffin?"

"One question at a time, my love." He walked around her, sending a wide beam of lantern light into all the corners, just in case the cave held other secrets. "All those times I sneaked truth serum into your tea and you never divulged one thing. I was sure you wouldn't be of any help to me, so I decided to fake my own death and kill you so I could gain access to all your worldly goods."

"Who was buried in your grave?" she demanded.

The body was already in the trunk before the accident. I made sure the guy's face was unrecognizable, that way if I wanted to come back again and claim the family belongings of my dearly departed wife I could."

"How could you explain that, if your body wasn't in the car?"

"I had built up lots of evidence that you were having an affair. It was your lover in that car. I would have just said I went to Europe to recover from my pain, and didn't realize you'd died until after the funeral."

"That's reprehensible."

He grinned at her. "Think so? You don't know me at all, my pet. He let one hand slide up the side of her face and she backed away from his touch. "But you survived the accident. I actually thought you were dead when I left or I would have finished the job myself. You put a crimp in my plans when you lived. And Brimm was getting more and more insistent that Vincent and I find the treasure, so we devised a way to get Sloan to lure you here."

So Brimm had known Sloan was an imposter all along. They'd been playing him, too. "Why?"

"He's an expert archaeologist. And he'd been making strides at regaining the family's good name within The Protectorate. We couldn't have that. The name deserves to die a flaming death. If we can't be members of The Protectorate, no Brockway can." He grinned and the lights cast shadows across his face making him look like the monster he was. "When you showed up again, it was an opportunity to find the treasure then kill both of you and blame Sloan for your death."

"You monster!"

He laughed. "Yeah, now you see why we deserved the kudos. My branch of the family is much more intelligent. We're the ones who have the guts to do what needs to be done."

She stared at him, he might look something like Sloan but his features were weaker. He had a weaker chin, shifty eyes and sly, drawn mouth that indicated his lack of faith in anything good.

"You used me. Victor told me I used to date Sloan. Even though I couldn't remember him, the familiarity of your face made me feel safe. That was why I thought I loved you. It was him I wanted, not you."

"Give me that ring, bitch." He grabbed at her hand that she tried to shove behind her back. "Have to say I'm a little disappointed that there wasn't more, but it is very valuable all by itself."

"How do you know that?"

His fingers dug into the soft flesh of her rotator cuff and she cried out. Her arm went limp and he peeled the ring off her thumb and stared at it lasciviously. "Because I found information in Phil's house before he died so tragically. Information about King Arthur's reign." He made a tisking sound and she wanted to scream. "Must be worth a fortune since it's supposed to belong to King Arthur."

She gasped. "It can't be. That's just a legend."

"Legend? Not likely. The stupid Protectorate kept the truth hidden for God only knows what reasons." He looked around the room again, his angry expression very similar to Barry's. "It's disappointing that they chose to leave only one item. But, it'll have to do, for now. "

"And who gets the money for the ring?" she asked. She knew him too well.

"That's something you'll never know, dearest, because unfortunately you're going to die alone in the dark in this secret chamber that your family created."

"You can't do that!"

"Watch me." He turned and fled up the stairs.

Heart palpitating, she scrambled up the steps behind him. Being locked inside this crypt and left to die became the driving force to escape. Unreleased air burned inside her lungs, and her chest tightened while she grabbed at him to stop him. She should have expected him to get physical, but it still surprised her when he kicked her backwards.

She tumbled down the wooden steps and landed in a heap at the bottom. The boulder closed over the opening before she could get off the ground again.

The only thought in her mind was that they would kill Sloan next. She couldn't help him. She was going to die, alone in the dark and he'd die on Jason Brimm's yacht because she'd failed him. She wished she could've told Sloan how she really felt about him first. If only she had remembered him. If only she could have trusted the feelings he elicited in her.

Something creepy-crawly slithered across her hand. She shook it off and screamed. Since her voice didn't echo inside this little room, the scream died quickly in the stagnant air.

Panicked for about two minutes before the will to survive kicked in, her first instinct was to check for any latches near the top of the steps. Surely there was a way to open the rock if it closed? After searching every crevice and crack she found nothing. She descended the stairs and sat on the ground next to the lantern with her knees pulled to her chest. The earth was cold and damp, and she prayed that no more bugs crawled on her. Another thought made her skin crawl—how long would the batteries last in the lantern? The hardest thing she'd ever done was turn off the light and face the cloying, inky black of the tiny room, to save power.

She pressed her forehead against her knees and tried to

figure a way out of this mess.

How long would they let Sloan live after Barry got back to the yacht? Without even considering the creepy crawlies, she dug her fingers into the damp sand and she leaned limply against one arm.

A soft flicker across her skin made her jump and she shook her hand. What had it been this time? A spider? Hold on, that feeling hadn't been caused by an insect. She put her hand back in the same spot and waited. Another flicker, a cool draft brushed her hand—it was air coming in from somewhere, a draft moving across the floor.

She snapped the lantern back on. Where was it coming from? It seemed cool air blew in at regular intervals. There was an opening somewhere in this room. How could she have given up? Her parents had created this place. That meant they'd have a safety net, and she already knew what she'd look for, a switch similar to the one in the basement. This room had a way out!

It took over an hour before she found another expertly hidden switch. She felt the whoosh of stale air mixed with fresh as the stone door opened into a tunnel that hadn't been used for a very long time. The tunnel was full of roots and webs and she had to crawl through the tangling vines, ignoring what she thought might be crawling through her hair or up her back.

After twenty feet or so, the tunnel opened into another small chamber with another series of tunnels going in every direction.

She had to hurry and find the boat. It might already be too late for Sloan because now that Barry had the ring, Sloan's time might be running out.

Had she ever been in this chamber before? There was a faint whistling sound ahead of her, no doubt caused by wind blowing through a crevice. That meant fresh air and maybe a way out.

She took that tunnel. Her instincts were good. No— they were great!

She found the boat room and climbed aboard Sloan's boat, untied it from the dock and started the engine. She'd watched him start it up the last time, so she knew how. Sweat glistened on her brow while she slowly propelled the boat through the cave opening into the fresh ocean air and the night. Stars twinkled in the heavens and she quickly spotted the offshore lights on the yacht moored a couple of miles off the island.

The moon cast a fractured silver ribbon across the undulating blackness of the ocean. A shiver racked her spine. She'd have to shove that fear aside in order to help Sloan.

If she tried to get near the yacht in the boat, they'd hear her. Her hopefulness slid to another bout of near panic. Sloan's life depended on her ability to be like her parents, brave and capable. They'd raised her for this, and she'd chosen the scared, cowardly route. Did she have the guts to live up to the standards they'd always hoped she'd have?

Maybe she did have what it took. Maybe she always had. After all, she'd grabbed the wheel when Barry had tried to kill her. She'd fought for life then and she'd do it again. She'd do it for Sloan, too. Saving him would either get her killed or give her back a reason to live. Reason to hold her head high and prove to the world that she was the Delacoeur's progeny in every way possible.

Her heart squeezed, but mostly she had to save Sloan, and maybe in doing so, she'd save herself.

But, how could she get to the yacht without being heard. She cut the engine a mile off the bow and scrounged around until she found the button to drop the anchor. She waited, a mental clock ticking off the moments in her head while the chain lowered. Could they hear it? Probably not. There was no sign that they knew she was here, a dot in the ocean beyond them.

Raven inhaled the salt air and tried to come to terms with what she had to do next. She had to get to the yacht, climb aboard without them hearing her and there was only one way to accomplish that.

Taking a long breath, she stripped off her jacket and looked at the waves moving between herself and the yacht. It was a given that those black undulating claws were waiting to grab her and haul her to the bottom if she fell in. She froze, fear debilitating her until she thought about Sloan, thought about how he'd offered to give the monsters anything as long as they let her live.

She could do this! She had to.

Thankfully, the moon provided the light she needed to see in the dark. Even from here she could see a rope ladder on the bow of the yacht. It was the only way for her to possibly get aboard unnoticed.

Unexpectedly, the sound of another boat approached from somewhere on the island. She hunkered down in her seat in hopes they wouldn't spot her. She gritted her teeth and held onto the steering wheel.

The boat sped up to the yacht without anyone noticing her. Within minutes it had docked and two men boarded the yacht. It was Barry she was sure of it. He must've been in the house while she made her escape.

Barry and the other man went into the galley. She saw several shadows through the portholes. With no idea how to get to Sloan if he was below deck, she took off her shoes and slipped over the side and into the icy black water that took her breath away—into the freezing cold ocean without a heart. At first she couldn't breathe and she started to panic. She went under. Twice.

She sputtered and coughed and cursed at herself under her breath. With the image of Sloan's guilty face when he tried to explain how his family had ruined her life, she started swimming. He couldn't die without knowing she didn't blame him for his relative's deeds. He'd proven he wasn't like them.

The only way she'd get through this was to focus on Sloan. She pictured him in her mind. Hurt. Needing her. She sucked in several deep breaths and began swimming toward the yacht again. Almost halfway there her reason failed and fear took over. What the hell was she doing? She looked back at his sleek speedboat.

She'd come too far to go back and she couldn't scream. Terror welled up inside her. Her arms suddenly went slack and she slipped under.

Panic made air escape from her lungs as she fought against the dark ocean and her fear. It was only her body's will to survive that brought her back to the surface, combating fear and craving the oxygen she so badly needed.

Her head broke the surface and she choked on the salt water she'd swallowed and inhaled. A wave splashed into her face and she choked down more salt water. She was shivering.

It felt as if spikes were being driven into her skull while memories suddenly came crashing back. Horrifying images of her parents being murdered and thrown into the ocean played out in her mind. Jagged, searing images that physically elicited pain she could only equate to the worst kind of migraine.

Her parents hadn't drowned. They'd been shot. Then she'd been tossed into the water beside their floating bodies. Her parents always made her wear a life jacket onboard. That was the only thing that saved her. Victor didn't shoot her because he never expected her to survive the cold water, and the deep ocean.

He'd never expected a fisherman to find her suffering from hypothermia and nearly dead. Now, she remembered her uncle coming to the hospital, the sadness in his eyes and her inability to tell him what had happened. She'd blocked it out. It had been too painful for her young mind to recall.

She choked on another mouthful of saltwater as she started to slip under again. The memory of her parents floating in the ocean, their blank eyes staring and not seeing before they sank out of sight. She remembered it all now. She had tried to keep them afloat. Tried to stop them from disappearing into the black, unforgiving nothingness of the horrible ocean.

Tears mixed with the saltwater. She turned herself over and floated on her back for a moment. She'd worn herself out fighting the ocean and her demons at the same time. If she didn't regain her strength, she would drown this time for good. And that wouldn't help Sloan. She owed him, big time!

While she floated, she knew what she had to do. And she couldn't let Victor Brockway win this time.

* * * * *

The fact that Sloan's hands were numb made it harder to get the knots loosened. To his advantage, one of the men had opened the porthole making it possible for him to hear what they were saying inside. And he didn't like what was being said.

"That bitch is not coming back this time," Barry said, and the others laughed. "I left her in a crypt of the Delacoeur's own making. She won't get out of that hole. She'll die there and I'll miraculously reappear and get what's coming to me. There has to be more of this treasure somewhere. It's obviously not on that damned island."

Sloan's heart slammed against his ribs and a gut-tearing urge to kill that bastard surged through him. "Oh, Raven," he moaned quietly as he let his muscles relax. He'd been tied up too tight to get away. How could he possibly escape?

He remained calm long enough to let some blood flow back into his fingers, then he started to work the ropes that were slashing his wrists to raw meat.

He had to find a way. "Raven…" he said quietly.

"Sloan? You called?"

It was Raven. He couldn't believe his ears. Or was he hearing things? Suddenly cold, shivering fingers were working at the knots on his wrists behind his back. It hurt like hell but he had to get them off.

"Oh, my God, Raven! You're alive? How'd you do it? I heard Barry say he buried you alive," Sloan whispered.

"No offence, but your cousin was never too bright. I found another way out."

"I'd kiss you right now if we didn't need to get our ass off this boat and the sooner the better," he said. His first hand came free and the blood surged back into it causing prickling pain.

"Hold still," she said and worked to free his other hand from the rope connected to his feet.

"I didn't hear a boat," he whispered, aching to taste her lips.

Her mouth was close to his ear now. "That's the whole idea. Otherwise, my husband and his lovely friends would have formed a welcoming committee."

"You swam? But how did you do it? You're terrified of the water."

"Terrified, yes, but I'm a strong swimmer due to another of my parents' training sessions when I was young and before my fear of the ocean took over."

She hesitated and gave him a look that twisted his insides. "I remember everything, Sloan. I remember when Victor killed my parents. He shot them then threw the three of us into the ocean. He thought I'd drown or die of hypothermia so he didn't bother shooting me."

"That sick Bastard!" Sloan's hand knotted up so tight the rope cut into his flesh anew. He could only imagine what it would do to a young girl to see her parents shot before her eyes, then to be left in the ocean with their dead bodies. No wonder she'd hidden from the world until recently.

"Unclench your fist. I'll never get the rope untied this way," she said.

A round of laughter erupted inside the galley and Sloan quickly relaxed his hand. He needed to be free of the ropes if he hoped to get Raven safely out of here.

She was working at his feet now, while he clenched and unclenched his fingers to get blood moving in his hands.

"There, that's the last knot," she whispered.

He could feel her fingers shaking against his skin. From the cold, or from the horrific experience in the ocean, he wasn't sure but he loved the fact that she'd been brave enough to save him.

He rubbed his ankles quickly and closed his eyes for a second. "I thought I'd lost you."

"Barry got the artifact," she said, not meeting his gaze.

"Who the hell cares about that? All I care about is you, Raven. If he'd done anything to you, I swear I would've made him pay, somehow."

"My parents and yours gave everything to protect those artifacts, Sloan. Can we really be so cavalier about a traitor stealing them for his own purposes?"

Pins and needles abating, Sloan pushed himself off the deck and stood. He couldn't stop himself from wrapping her in his arms, if only for a second. She was dripping and she felt like ice.

Next he kissed her quickly and grabbed her hand. "Yes, we can. You ready to get out of here, my love?"

She nodded, but he could feel the muscles in her back

tightening at the prospect of diving into that horrible ocean again. He gritted his teeth and squeezed her hand to give her the continued strength. "You're an amazing, woman, Raven. You've risen above what would have crippled most people. You can do this."

* * * * *

Before they had a chance to get off the boat, a flash of lightning streaked across the sky and thunder rumbled in the distance. Nimbostratus clouds slid across the night sky partially blocking out the moonlight.

"Great weather for a swim," Sloan said, not realizing that Raven's tension level had elevated by about a thousand.

Not only did she have to get back into the black depths that threatened to suck her under, but now the whole thing would be a huge conduit to lightning.

They'd barely reached the ladder when someone shouted behind them. "He's getting away!"

"Hurry, either dive or get down the ladder," Sloan said.

"Sloan, I… I can't."

He gently touched the small of her back, urging her forward in jerky movements. She grabbed onto the rail. "You go first."

"Nope. You go first or we both stay."

"Stop right there, you two," Jason Brimm said from the deck above. His Magnum pointed at them menacingly.

"Oh no, if I'd jumped into the water we would have gotten away," she said, pressing her face into Sloan's shoulder. "This is my fault."

"No, honey," he said, pulling her to his side and protecting her from the line of fire. "You've been amazing and brave. We wouldn't have gotten far in the water anyway. They would've just fished us out—or…" He let the words trail off.

She knew what he was going to say. Shoot them. Just like Victor had done to her parents, before he'd left her to drown.

Suddenly the deck lit up and a spotlight focused on them. Barry, Victor and Brimm's two henchmen approached with guns aimed at them.

"My, my, you got out of that dank hole I left you in, my darling," Barry said. Even though he tried to keep his voice light, Raven could hear the irritation in it. "You must have nine lives."

Brimm stomped down the spiral stairs from the upper deck and glared at Barry. "You're becoming a useless waste of skin. The last time you tried to kill her, you failed, and now you've failed again."

Victor pushed ahead of Barry. "The bitch has nine lives, it's not Barry's fault. I think it proves she knows more about the island than she's letting on, don't you, Brimm?"

Brimm considered Victor's statement and his gaze seared hers before turning on Barry again. "This screw-up makes me wonder what else your brother has failed at, Victor?" Brimm held up his hand, indicating the stolen ring glistening on his pinky finger. "Was this really the only artifact in the caves? Is your loser brother mistaken again, or maybe keeping the treasure for himself?"

Barry's face turned a mottled shade of purple and he started to push past Victor to get at Brimm. Victor held his brother back with one extended arm.

"Don't be an idiot Barry," he said.

"I'm getting tired of this effing bastard, Vic. We're the ones with the knowledge, and these clowns think they're better'n us. They're nothin' but glorified hoods."

Raven watched Brimm's reaction to her husband's comment and realized Barry was poking a mean dog without considering the outcome. She had the feeling he'd done that his whole life, but he'd most likely met his match this time, at least that's what she'd hoped until Brimm's beady-eyed gaze returned to her and Sloan.

"Better tell me now if this little ring is the only thing being protected on that island," he said practically baring his teeth. "The more I think of it, I can't imagine using a whole island and massive caves to hide a tiny ring and nothing else."

"That's all there was," Raven said.

"I think you're lying," Brimm accused. "Perhaps you're in cahoots with your dearly departed husband in order to cut me out of my share?"

"I wouldn't lift one finger to save him." She cast a disgusted look at Barry. She thought his bravado looked a little forced right now and she didn't feel one bit sorry for him.

"Keep your cool," Sloan said under his breath, wrapping his hand around hers.

Victor jumped in. "I spent the last eight years searching through those damned caves. There's nothing there. The Delacoeur's must've moved everything before they died. The only things left were those crates and they were all empty. They must've dropped the ring by mistake when they moved the rest out."

"Before you killed them, you mean. I can't believe you did such an idiotic thing before you found out where the treasure was," Brimm said.

Raven surreptitiously glanced at Sloan. His mouth was set in a grim line while he assessed their situation, she could tell he was trying to come up with a plan to save them.

It irked her that Victor thought he knew where everything was. He hadn't even found the secret room in Uncle Phil's house and wouldn't have been able to get inside if he had.

Her parents had done their job very well. For the first

time she understood their incentive to do this job. It got into a person's blood.

But that still created a problem for The Protectorate. They didn't know where the treasures were either, and that ring was the tip of the iceberg. There was more. Lots more. Since her near drowning episode her memories were slowly filtering back and somewhere in the clouded perceptions of her youth, she remembered sitting at an ancient table surrounded by knight's armor. Each suit of armor held the same crest as the one on the ring.

She'd been in the treasure room! It was really there.

Her hand squeezed Sloan's and her heart pounded in her chest. Sloan took his eyes off the quarreling men in front of him long enough to see why Raven had squeezed his hand. His eyebrows rose quizzically at her sudden excitement.

"We've got to get off this boat," she whispered. "I think I know where it is."

"Holy mother!" Sloan turned his attention back to the pack of men waging a war of wills in front of them with a firestorm about to erupt. No matter which way things went, the outcome would be grim for them. He had to control this situation somehow. He watched and waited for his chance to get the upper hand.

Treasure or not, his objective had always been to get Raven out of this mess first and foremost. His gut clenched. He loved her. He wanted to have a life with her. But she'd never be able to forgive him for his cousin's treachery and he didn't blame her.

"This ring might be King Arthur's," Brimm said angrily. "But it's not worth much without some kind of proof. That means I've spent a shitload of money on your searches and you've come up short."

Victor's nervous gaze shifted back and forth between

Brimm and his henchmen. Meanwhile, Barry didn't seem to pick up on their dangerous situation. Sloan always knew the guy was an idiot, but this clinched it.

"You know where you can stick it," Barry said to Brimm. Everyone started shouting at once with Brimm's men facing off against Victor and Barry. Sloan edged Raven slowly sideways, hoping no one would notice. A shot fired and Sloan grabbed Raven and dove off the side of the ship. They plunged under the water. He held Raven's hand but she fought his grasp.

He pulled her to the surface and gave her a chance to breathe. "Raven, swim and keep swimming no matter what happens."

Another shot fired from the deck into the water beside them. Several more shots were fired.

She swam at first but stopped and began to tread water when they were out of range of the yacht. "I can't," she said. "I'm too tired."

Sloan treaded water beside her and asked, "Where's the boat? You used mine, right?"

She coughed when a wave slapped her in the face. "I don't know where it is. It should be nearby."

Sloan scanned the ocean around them. They'd gone a distance from the Yacht, but still had quite a swim to shore. The anchor must not have grabbed, or it didn't hit the bottom. The speedboat was gone.

He turned back to Raven and she was gone. "Holy shit, Raven!" he shouted and dove under the pitch-black water. He couldn't see her. He started reaching, grabbing, in order to find her. No way would he give up.

If her hair hadn't been floating above her body, he might have missed her all together. He touched her hair, wrapped his fingers into it and reached down to grab her and pulled her back to the surface. When she broke the surface she started coughing.

Luckily he was a strong swimmer. He held her with

one arm, and stroked toward shore with the other.

They were both exhausted by the time they reached shore. He dragged her out of the water and dropped her gently before he sagged onto the beach next to her, his head resting against her shoulder.

"You okay, doll?" he asked. He'd nearly let her drown. He couldn't believe he'd been so stupid.

She turned her head to his. "I have the feeling I'll always be okay as long as you're around." Her cold, wrinkled fingertips stroked the side of his face making him feel warmth in the middle of near hypothermia.

In the distance, the sound of helicopter rotor blades brought Sloan's head up off the sand. "Damn it, they've called for reinforcements. We've got to get out of here," Sloan said.

Raven, pushed up onto one elbow. "It might be your Protectorate," she said. "I phoned Johnson before I came to get you. I found your SAT phone in the boat."

He took her face in his hands. "You're the most amazing woman I've ever met. If you could ever forgive me for being related to Victor and Barry, I would do everything in my power to make you happy." He stared into the depths of her eyes. "I love you with all my heart."

"You're the boy under the tree in my back yard, aren't you?"

That question surprised him. He nodded. "You remember?"

She looked him over. "I should have remembered the first time I saw you. Why didn't I?" They'd dated and she'd loved him then, just as she loved him now.

He laughed. "And I was a gangly teenager, you were an unqualified beauty even back then," he said.

He helped her to her feet and they leaned against each other. The helicopter got closer. A spotlight found them and the helicopter landed nearby. Two men from The

Protectorate ran to them. Since she was barely able to stand, Sloan kept her on her feet. Two more helicopters circled the yacht.

"We got 'em," Sloan." A burley man dressed in fatigues said. "Thanks to you and Raven," he smiled at her like he knew her.

"Raven, this is John Ernst. He's one of the new Triumvirates."

"Hello," she said.

He smiled at her and took her hand and shook it then said, "Hop into the bird, we'll go to the yacht. Victor and his band of merry men should be in handcuffs by now."

As predicted, everyone on the yacht had been handcuffed by a tactical team that looked like some sort of special ops group. Raven wouldn't want to mess with them. They actually looked meaner than Brimm's men. Barry wouldn't even glance at her while he was being loaded into a helicopter with Victor and Brimm. That didn't bother her one bit, because for the first time since the accident, he really was dead to her. Her need to know had been satisfied and she never wanted to see him again.

John Ernst spoke into headgear he was wearing. "Take them to headquarters for questioning. I'll expect some results by the time I return tomorrow."

Raven had been sitting on a bench seat on the deck watching everything play out. She heard what John Ernst had said and she looked at Sloan. "Why aren't they being arrested by the FBI?"

"I'm actually surprised, myself," he said. "I don't understand why they haven't called the FBI."

John Ernst must have been listening because he said, "The Protectorate will turn them over as soon as they make sure they don't divulge anything they shouldn't."

Raven started to speak but Sloan secretly squeezed her arm.

"Yes, Mrs. Gale? What do you want to know?" Ernst

said.

"Nothing," she said.

He sat down beside her. "Tell me, are there any other artifacts left on that island? If so, you need to tell me now, they belong to The Protectorate."

An odd sensation buzzed through her. Something about this conversation didn't feel right. "No, there was nothing else there," she said and flashed a quick look at Sloan wondering how he'd react to her answer. She'd told him she knew where the treasure was hidden.

Sloan's expression remained blank, corroborating her statement. "We searched that place top to bottom, wherever Raven's parents hid the stuff, it wasn't on that island."

John got up close and too personal. Raven didn't like the greed she saw behind his façade. His salt and pepper hair, expensive designer glasses and overly white teeth didn't surprise her; everything about him seemed like a prop to give him credibility. He wanted that treasure, and she wasn't sure his motives were any different than Brimm or Barry.

"You're absolutely sure?" he asked.

"Positive," she said. She was positive. This man wasn't to be trusted.

Anger flickered, but he managed to hide it quickly. "Well, I'm sorry to hear that but I would like to take this moment to welcome you to our group. You were born to be a member, and we'd be proud to have you."

She flicked at quick glance toward Sloan. It seemed the invitation was for her only. That ticked her off even more. While Sloan's expression remained unreadable, she imagined he was seething under the surface.

"Thanks," she said. "I'll have to think about it and get back to you."

The unctuous smile wiped of Ernst's face and he instantly frowned at Sloan, as if any of this was his fault.

"What can we do to convince you to join us, Ms. Delacoeur?" He placed his hand on her shoulder and she edged out from under it.

So, he'd used her maiden name this time. That was the truth of it, he wanted her because of her name and because she might find their treasure.   Raven swallowed and considered her parents being a member of this group. There was no way they'd have been part and party to a group like this. She could only assume the people who'd taken over after the previous Triumvirate had been assassinated, weren't quite so altruistic. She needed to discuss the matter with Sloan in private.

"Like I said, I'll have to think about it." She managed to smile at him and soothe his fears. When he wasn't looking, she planned to run the other way. "I've been through a lot this week. I need to figure a few things out first."

John shook his head. "Of course you do, I'm sorry for trying to press you it's just that we've all been so excited about reinstating a Delacoeur into our midst." Again, there was no mention of Sloan.

He rubbed his hands together and she noticed that King Arthur's ring now sparkled on his baby finger. He'd found the loot and he was wearing it!   Would an upstanding member of The Protectorate do that?

"Would you mind flying Sloan and me back to the island?" she asked. She took Sloan's hand and held it tight. His fingers immediately interlaced with hers. She daren't leave him behind with this crew. She didn't trust them. If they wanted to trick her into their secret group, they might leave him alone for now.

John's face cracked a smile. His eyes glittered. "Of course."

Not once did he make eye contact with Sloan that she could tell.

Sloan climbed into the helicopter behind her and they

disembarked in the field near the house. Neither of them said a word during the flight. The pilot left them in the field in the dark, the ear shattering sounds of his chopper blades ruining the ambiance of this place. Still sopping wet and shivering they made for the house.

"Let's get inside and have a hot shower," she said. She thought that might get a rise out of him, but he merely nodded his head.

"Sloan, we need to talk," she said the minute they got inside the old house.

He pressed a finger over his mouth and reached out to pull a little device off the collar of her shirt. He carefully laid it on the table in the hallway.

"I know what you're going to say," he said, his eyes warning her to go along with everything. "That you were right all along and there's nothing here in this house."

"I know," she said, following his lead. "I can't believe we had to go through so much for a measly ring. I can't wait to get home and put this whole thing behind me."

"Let's get some sleep and head out early in the morning."

"Good idea."

He led her into the bathroom and turned the shower on full blast, then ran the sink taps, as well. "Looks like The Protectorate our parents worked for is a thing of the past."

He already knew she'd figured that out. Her heart swelled. "But what is their agenda? Why do they want King Arthur's treasure? Just for the money?"

His eyes widened. "King Arthur?"

She nodded and smiled.

"Wow, I hadn't expected that. I thought Ernst was wrong when he said the ring belonged to King Arthur. It's real?"

She nodded again.

"About The Protectorate, there's something nefarious

going on inside the group."

"Like what?"

"I don't know. But I do know our parents would be turning over in their graves to see their beloved Protectorate being run by people like those we saw tonight."

She put the lid down on the flush and sat, he sat on the edge of the tub next to her. "What are we going to do about it?"

His eyebrows rose. "What do you mean?"

"Are we going to just sit back and let them ruin a society that existed for the betterment of mankind, or are we going to make sure they don't succeed?"

He laughed and grabbed the back of her head and pulled her to him. He kissed her long and hard. "You're the woman of my dreams, doll."

"And you're the man of mine," she said. "I've missed you so much. I love you, Sloan."

"Are you just saying that, or do you really remember?"

"Oh, I remember a gawky young man whose kisses weren't quite as sophisticated as they are now."

He smiled against her mouth and kissed her again. She melted into them, and wanted more, so much more. But that would have to wait. They had an assignment. A job that only they could do and it involved an adventure that even her parents would relish.

Somehow, she'd managed to get through it all and come full circle. Now, she couldn't imagine any other life. The steam from the shower felt great, still she shivered and picked a piece of seaweed out of her hair.

Sloan stood, and running a hand along her jaw line, drew her to her feet. "You shower first and then we'll talk. If I get into that shower with you right now I won't be able to keep my mind on what we have to do to get away from here without Protectorate interference." He smiled into her eyes and in the depths she saw the truth. He loved her.

"Rain check?" he asked.

"Definitely," she said.

They got up at the crack of dawn the next morning and ate breakfast, all the while, aware that part of the house was under surveillance. Someone was listening.

Didn't matter, Sloan couldn't remember the last time he'd been this happy.

The radio blasted them the whole time they ate breakfast. A breaking news broadcast stopped them cold. A helicopter had gone down in the Bay of Fundy yesterday with four men aboard. Barry Brockway, Victor Brockway, Jason Brimm and the pilot Rob Kent were all killed upon impact.

Sloan quickly turned to Raven, she looked stunned. Finally, she shook her head and said, "He tempted fate, and now he's truly dead."

"I'm sorry it ended like this, though, Raven. It would have been better to see him pay for his crimes."

"Oh, I think he paid," she said, getting up quietly and snagging a piece of paper from the counter near the sink. She wrote a quick note. Sloan read it silently and nodded. He followed her to the basement. They opened the secret door and entered the tunnels. There were no listening devices down here.

"Follow me," she said. "The cave opening is over there."

"I'm on your six."

"Huh?"

"Never mind," he grinned. "I'm right behind you."

Inside the cave she stopped for a moment and took his hands. She peered into his face with a guilty expression he didn't understand.

"I have to tell you something. I think I married Barry because there was a weak resemblance to you, Sloan. Even though I had no memory of that time in my life, I was searching for you, the man I'd fallen in love with when I was a girl of sixteen."

Sloan's mouth came down on hers. He wanted to press her against the wall right now and sink his fingers into her glossy hair, taste her mouth. He'd do that later, they didn't have time right now. He didn't trust The Protectorate and if they were silent for too long, someone might come looking for them.

"I tried to see you once after you moved in with your Uncle Phil. He told me if I really loved you I had to stay away." Sloan gritted his teeth. "I knew at that time what he'd said was true. You weren't ready for the whole truth, it would have torn you apart. No matter how much I needed you, I had to protect you from further pain."

"And yet we found each other again," she sniffed, and pressed her face against his neck.

"You found me, lady," he said with a grin. "And it took a lot of strength to do what you did." He swiped a few tendrils from her forehead. "Not to mention swimming to the yacht to save me."

She shuddered. "I did that, didn't I? Do you think the helicopter crash was an accident?" she whispered, even though she probably didn't have to.

He nodded. "I sure hope so. I don't want to think the men running The Protectorate right now are that brutal."

"What's going to happen to The Protectorate? Will they continue to become an evil empire? What's their agenda?"

Sloan smiled. "The Protectorate has been around for hundreds of years. They've had to deal with issues like this before. These men will be dealt with."

Raven looked puzzled. "But how?

"The main branch of The Protectorate is European. They know what's been going on here, and they have undercover operatives gathering information. There's enough information now to address these problems."

"What does that mean?"

"A tribunal will be held. The offenders will go to prison."

"Regular prison?"

He shrugged his shoulders. "Sometimes good groups that work for the betterment of mankind have to keep their own prisoners."

"The Protectorate?"

He nodded.

"How do you know all of this?"

"Because the oldest most respected families, including yours have always been members of the European sector. Most North American members don't know that, it's part of the safety net that keeps our society secure."

She shook her head and smiled at him. "I can't believe it. You're still one of them, aren't you? You were never really cast out from the group, you went underground to find out who'd betrayed the North American sector of The Protectorate."

"You're quick, Ms. Delacoeur." He kissed the tip of her nose.

He watched her quickly assimilate the new information. He loved that about her. She was clever.

She looked at him out of the corner of her eye and held out her hand. "So, d'you wanna see the real treasure room?"

He grinned at her. His heart nearly burst at her show of faith. "I sure do, but there's nothing I'll ever treasure more than you."

# # #

Message from the Author

Thank you for investing that most precious of commodities – your time—in my book! If you enjoyed What She Doesn't Know, I would be thrilled if you could help me buzz it. You can do this by:

Recommending it: Help other readers find this book by recommending it to friends, readers' groups and discussion board.

Reviewing it. Please share with other readers what you liked about this book by reviewing it wherever you purchased it, or at readers' sites such as GoodReads.

If you do choose to review it, I would be delighted to thank you publicly on my **blog**.

I love hearing from readers. Feel free to **email me at lina@linagardiner.com**.

Scroll down to read an excerpt from another romantic suspense, Unknown Assailant.

About the Author

Lina Gardiner, author of the award winning Jess Vandermire Vampire Hunter Series has writing in her blood. Living in New Brunswick, Canada, a hotspot for legendary ghosts and tall tales of odd happenings has probably added to her love of a good mystery. That, and the stories her grandfather told in the "parlor" when their grandmother wasn't paying attention, added to her love of storytelling, and the wonders of imagination.

Winner of the Prism Award, Best First Book, from FF&P (Futuristic, Fantasy and Paranormal Chapter of RWA).

Nominee for the Romantic Times Reviewer's Choice Best Book Awards.

Nominee for the Paranormal Romance Guild Reviewers' Choice Awards.

Her books have been well received by such reviewers as Kirkus Reviews and USA Today's HEA blog, including a 4.5-star rating from RT Book Reviews.

Acknowledgements

Special thanks to Nola Richardson, my best friend, who always has time for me and for proofreading when I need it. Smooch!

Other Books

Romantic Suspense
Unknown Assailant

Paranormal Romance / Urban Fantasy
Jess Vandermire, Vampire Hunter Series
Grave Illusions (Book 1)
Beyond the Grave (Book 2)
Grave New Day (Book 3)
Grave Expectations (Book 4)

Dangerous Exposure
Black Moon Awakening

Fantasy / Dystopian
Gift of Prophecy

Excerpt – Unknown Assailant

By Lina Gardiner

Copyright © Lina Gardiner 2014

EVERY NIGHT after work, Liz Davis parked her car in front of the two-story white house accented with black shutters and glistening red door. A lump formed in her throat. This picture-perfect exterior couldn't have been further from the truth. And now, to make everything worse, she'd gotten fired today.

Dry leaves leftover from last fall rustled on the lawn, making the skin tingle on the back of her neck. Thickening shadows near the shrubbery next to the garage door made her search for shapes that shouldn't be there. With the latest rash of vandalism, she'd been rattled. Luckily, the shadows were just shadows.

She opened the front door and relocked it the second she got inside. Her parents had died in a car accident a year ago and her world had gone haywire ever since. Maybe she was actually losing her mind because she'd swear someone was trying to deliberately scare her.

Her anxiety had cost her her job. Not that she'd ever fit in there. She'd been too preoccupied to do a half-decent job as a front store manager.

Two days ago the police department had closed the year-old file on her parents' deaths. The ruling stated the motor vehicle crash had been an accident.

She'd reminded the investigator about the acts of vandalism still happening to her. She'd personally phoned the police on several occasions for flat tires, broken windows, and other incidents.

She'd seen the same look in the officer's eyes that she'd seen in her co-workers' expressions. Everyone thought she was making it all up to keep her parents' file open.

She'd had no luck trying to contact her uncle since her parents had died and now she was alone. No friends, no family, and no one to turn to.

Going down the hallway into the kitchen, she made for the teakettle. A hot cup of tea would soothe her nerves. She let out a shaky breath and wondered what she'd do now. No job. The police didn't believe her, and she didn't feel safe in her own home.

She flicked the switch on the electric kettle—her hand barely touched the ceramic mug on the first shelf when the lights snapped out. She jumped and knocked a mug onto the granite counter top, where it shattered instantly. She heard and felt the tiny shards bouncing off the counter.

That thought left her quickly because silence buzzed the room like a three-alarm fire. She froze where she stood. Had the power just gone out? Or was something else going on?

She held her breath for a few seconds then let it out slowly. Crap! No wonder her co- workers thought she was crazy. Everything seemed like a conspiracy to her. She'd just managed to turn a mere power outage into something much worse in her mind.

She'd heard rumbling off in the distance a few minutes ago. There'd been a thunderstorm threatening all day. Lightning must have struck a pole nearby.

Feeling her way along the counter to her miscellaneous drawer, she opened it and started to feel around for a penlight. She'd use it to help find the bigger battery-operated lantern in the hall closet.

A low, out-of-place creak in the hallway shattered the silence, and Liz stopped digging. Oh God! Someone was in her house.

A scream rose in her throat, until a gust of wind buffeted the side of her house, causing another creak. Liz swallowed hard and cursed herself for her stupidity. Deep thunder rolled in the distance. The storm was coming fast, and with it stronger wind.

She released a shaky breath. She was alone in the house. Alone, and afraid of the dark, apparently. "Get a grip on yourself, Liz," she mumbled, beginning to forage again for the flashlight. Where the heck was it?

Thunder rumbled again. Closer this time. She'd almost convinced herself everything was okay when the hall floorboard creaked again, a sound that rang like a buzzer in her brain.

This time, it definitely hadn't been wind settling the house.

Those particular floorboards creaked only when someone stood in that hallway between the kitchen and the front door. And, she thought she smelled a faint odor of men's cologne.

Just feet away from her.

Her arms iced over, and her throat tightened. She streaked toward the back door off the kitchen.

"Stop, bitch," a deep male voice shouted. Out of the dark, a hand snagged the back of her shirt, then grabbed her hair and yanked her backward.

She screamed. It echoed through the house. But no one else lived here anymore. No one could help. She sobbed. "What do you want?" Her hands went to her hair to try to relieve the yanking pressure on her scalp. "Let me go."

His arms wrapped her in a tight squeeze and he ground himself against her and let out a guttural, disgusting sound.

If this was the person who'd been tormenting her for the last year, his incursions had escalated beyond mere vandalism. She was in deep trouble, and if she wanted to live, she'd better start fighting. Now!

She managed to smash him on the chin with her elbow. He grunted but locked her arms at her sides so she couldn't do it again. It was dark enough that she couldn't see anything but an outline. She wouldn't be able to identify him even if she survived this attack.

His fingers dug into the tender flesh on her arms, and she gritted her teeth against crying out again. No way did she intend to do anything to make this easy for him, but she'd have to be smart. She'd have to find a way to fight him off.

"Been waiting awhile for this," he said in a husky, nearly panting voice that scared her beyond words.

"I've got a present for you, little lady," the voice grated in her ear. He made a lurid, sexual sound, and then laughed. That laugh scared her more than the attack itself.

"Oh God, help me!" she screamed, before his hand clamped over her mouth. Tears sprang to her eyes as her chest exploded into a burning ball of pain from lack of oxygen. He'd started panting in her ear again—and then someone knocked on the front door.

He cursed under his breath and lessened his hold just enough for her to gasp for breath.

Until then, she'd barely registered that someone was insistently knocking on the front door.

"Shut up if you know what's good for you." He dragged her to the far corner of the kitchen.

A key grated in the lock, and the door opened. "Liz, are you in here?"

Only one person had a key to her house. The one person she trusted enough to have a key. Maggie Cranston, her next-door neighbor.

No, Maggie, run! Don't come in here! The unvoiced scream filled her head, but her captor kept his hand so tight over her mouth she felt she wasn't getting enough air.

Maggie advanced slowly, holding a lantern. She must have seen the power go out. Meanwhile, Liz's attacker pulled her farther back into the shadows. "Keep quiet, or you're both in trouble," he whispered.

"I saw the lights go out over here and thought I'd better come over and check on you," Maggie said in a perplexed voice. She paused, then took several steps down the hallway. "Liz? Where are you, dear?" She took a right turn, and the light disappeared into the living room.

With that vile hand clamped over her mouth, Liz couldn't shout, but she did try to struggle. Maggie started into the hallway again.

"Damn it all to hell!" he grated in her ear, then without warning, he shoved her down onto the kitchen floor and dashed out the back door.

Liz hit the floor hard, but managed to break her fall with her hands. Glass cut into her left palm. Her throat felt raw, and she couldn't make a noise.

Maggie had heard the commotion and rushed into the kitchen, bathing Liz in lantern light.

"Help." Liz barely managed to make her voice heard.

"Oh my dear! What happened? Have you broken something?" Maggie's facial features appeared ghoulish in the shadowy glow of her flashlight. Broken glass crunched when she set the flashlight on the floor beside Liz. "You're bleeding. You've cut your hand."

"Call the police," Liz managed to croak out.

"What?" Maggie looked bewildered.

Liz nodded vigorously, clutching her throat. "You just scared off an intruder! He was in my house waiting for me to come home."

"You're kidding." Maggie's chubby hand flew to her mouth. "When your lights went out and no one else's did, I thought you'd blown a breaker. I wasn't sure you knew where the fuse box was, so I came to help."

Liz rubbed her sore throat. What would he have done to her if Maggie hadn't shown up? She shivered at the thought. "Lucky for me you noticed."

Maggie helped her up and onto a kitchen chair. Her motherly fingers smoothed her mussed hair. "Stay right there, Liz, I'm going to call the police."

"Would you lock the back door first?"

"Oh geez!" Maggie ran to the door and pulled it shut and snapped the chain in place. Not that locked doors had kept out the intruder the first time. How had he gotten into her   home?
Maggie kept Liz grounded while they waited for the cops. Somehow it felt like it took forever, but a female officer arrived within twenty minutes and introduced herself as Officer Spencer.

"Tell me what happened," she said, holding a pen over her notepad.

Liz quickly gave her a rundown, and afterward her teeth and jaw ached from trying not to panic all over again.

"I see," the tall woman said, looking her over from head to toe. "Did he steal anything?"

"I don't think stealing was on his agenda," Liz said, unable to keep the quiver out of her voice.

"Oh, dear me." Maggie's hand was over her mouth again, and her eyes began watering. She had such a tender heart.

"I know how terrifying it must've been for you to encounter someone in your house, but most likely you interrupted a break-in," the officer said.

"No way in hell," Liz ground out and ran her hands through her tangled hair. "Given all the other things that have happened to me lately, this attack was personal." She couldn't believe the officer had just said that.

"Just take a minute to assess your situation, Ms. Davis," Officer Spencer began in a trained voice. "It's completely normal for a person to assume the worst when they come across an intruder, but sometimes intruders just want to get out of the house when they're caught. Maybe you got in his way? And, there have been a few break-ins in the neighborhood the last few weeks. If this is the same intruder, I don't think you have to worry about him coming back." She held up a hand and waved her pen, still lodged between two fingers. "Not that it's not a scary occurrence, but you need to understand it likely wasn't anything personal."

Liz couldn't believe what she was hearing. "But my brake line was cut last week. Why would a thief do that?"

The officer frowned. "Did you report it?"

Feeling defensive, Liz shot her an angry look. "Of course I did, and I've reported a few other incidents that happened over the last year. Someone is stalking me."

"Just a moment, I'd like to get your records on the brake incident," Officer Spencer said, pulling out her cell phone.

Surely they'd delve deeper into the incidents happening to her this time. Two attempts on her life. Wouldn't that be a little too obvious to ignore?

Officer Spencer stepped into the living room to make her call. She returned a couple of minutes later. "I've checked on the details of the brake incident. Apparently, there was no evidence of tampering." She regarded Liz. "Am I right?"

Liz wanted to scream. She was right! Damn it. She nodded.

"While I realize this incident seems connected to you, there's nothing to indicate it wasn't a random occurrence. As I said, there have been a lot of break-ins in the neighborhood recently. This guy was probably getting ready to rob you when you came in and spoiled his plans."

Liz's arms and legs felt like lead. Her attack hadn't been a foiled robbery, but there was no chance she'd convince the police of that. "So I've been the victim of two random crimes in two weeks? And it's all one big coincidence?"

"I know you want it to be something else, Ms. Davis, but you most likely caught someone attempting to rob you. I suggest you get your locks changed and consider staying with a friend for a while if you don't feel safe."

Easy to tell Officer Spencer had talked to Chief Hanlon. He'd been making her feel like a nut case since day one. Poor little distraught woman who couldn't face up to her parents' death. It wasn't that!

"And if you're wrong?" Something was going on, and no one believed her. Certainly not the police. She had little recourse. It was time she looked after herself.